HOLLYWOOD ROOMMATES

ELIZABETH BRIGGS

Copyright © 2018 by Elizabeth Briggs

HOLLYWOOD ROOMMATES: A Reverse Harem Romance

All rights reserved. This book or any portion thereof may not be reproduced or used in any manner whatsoever without the express written permission of the publisher except for the use of brief quotations in a book review.

This is a work of fiction. Names, characters, businesses, places, events and incidents are either the products of the author's imagination or used in a fictitious manner. Any resemblance to actual persons, living or dead, or actual events is purely coincidental.

Cover Designed by KassiJean Designs

Model Photo by Lindee Robinson Photography

Cover Model: Kelly Kirstein

ISBN (paperback) 978-1984203663

ISBN (ebook) 978-0991569670

www.elizabethbriggs.net

To Gary
For telling me to go for it

CHAPTER ONE

ALLIE

THE PROPOSAL IS COMING, I know it.

Parker, my sweet, handsome boyfriend, sits before me in a navy blue suit, the wind teasing at his dark, silky hair. The pink roses he brought me rest on the marble table beside our plates. Any second now he's going to pull out a ring and pop the question. Why else would he invite me to this specific restaurant for lunch?

We've been dating a year. Living together for six months. It's totally time.

"This past year has been really great, Allie," Parker says.

I smile at him and take a sip of my wine. "Yes, it has."

"And you're such a great person." He clears his throat and yanks on his tie, looking everywhere but me. He's obviously nervous. Of course he is. A proposal is a big deal.

I reach across the table and rest a hand over his. "Moving in with you was one of the best decisions I ever made. Some people thought it was too soon, but it felt right. Don't you think so?"

He slides his hand away. "Yeah. Um. It's been great."

Yes, I'm great, he's great, we're all great. Okay, so Parker isn't a master of words and clearly hasn't prepared this speech very well, but I can live with that. Everything else about him is perfect, after all. Or mostly perfect anyway. I mean, every couple has their problems, right?

Just when I start to wonder if he's ever going to get the nerve to do it, I spot a plane behind him. One of those small ones, flitting low across the cloudless blue sky, leaving a trail of white in its wake. As the waiter clears our plates, the plane slowly spells out the words, MARRY ME.

Hope spreads throughout my chest. It's happening. It's really happening.

I smile even wider at Parker, who chugs his wine like it's water and he's on a desert island. How adorably nervous he is. I look up again, and there, below it...

Is that an *A*?

I sit up straighter in my chair, my heart racing. No wonder he wanted to sit outside today. I had no idea Parker was such a romantic. This skywriting stunt totally makes up for his lack of preparing a speech.

"You were saying...?" I ask, although I can't stop looking at the letters forming behind his head. The next letter is an *L*, like in my name. This is it for sure. I want to kick my feet and squee.

Parker clears his throat. "Yeah. Um. Well. It's been a year and I think it's time we move on."

I nod. C'mon next letter! "Exactly. Move forward. Couldn't agree more."

"I care about you a lot."

"I care about you too." The plane draws a straight line. The start of another *L*?

"And I want you to be happy."

"Of course. I am. Happy, I mean."

"I just think that—"

There it is. A second *L*! I can't hold it in any longer. I jump to my feet and clasp my hands to my chest. "Yes, I'll marry you!"

He looks up at me with his mouth hanging open. "What?"

I sit back down with a giggle. "Sorry, I just got excited. I should have waited for you to ask me first." I smooth the skirt of my dress and smile at him. "Okay, I'm ready. Go for it."

His eyebrows pinch together, causing a deep line to form between them. "Why would you think I'm proposing?"

"This is the restaurant where we had our first date. You brought me flowers. And of course, there's that." I gesture to the skywriting behind him. The plane has already begun to form the next letter, which I know will be an *I*.

He turns in his chair to look. "Oh, shit."

Wait a second. Is that...an *E*?

Parker turns back around as a sour feeling hits my stomach. "Allie, I'm not proposing."

"You're not?" No, that can't be right. The pilot is clearly spelling my name wrong. Probably switching the *I* and the *E*. I stare up at the plane, hoping with everything I have that the letters will magically change.

"No. I'm trying to break up with you."

My eyes snap to his face. "What?"

"Listen, there's no good way to say this. I want to see other people. Well, one person. I met someone. At work."

"You...met someone." My head spins. The letter is definitely an *E*, not an *I*. Followed by another one that looks like it's going to be an *N*. No, no, no, that can't be right. This isn't how this lunch is supposed to go at all.

"I was trying to break it to you easily." Parker shakes his head. "Shit. I can't believe you thought I was proposing."

I stare at him, my mouth dry. Behind his head, the letters clearly spell a name that isn't my own. Somewhere nearby, a guy named Allen is getting engaged and I'm not.

When I can speak, my voice is small. "But the restaurant. The flowers."

"I completely forgot we went here on our first date. It's a convenient spot near my office, that's all. And I brought the flowers because I feel bad." He folds his hands on the table. "Especially because I need you to move out."

I reach for my glass of water, but his words shock me so much I knock it over. The water spreads across the table and onto Parker's lap. Who, frankly, kind of deserves it. "You want me to move out?"

He grabs a napkin, his mouth twisting in annoyance as he wipes at the water. "Yeah. By the end of the week. So Amy can move in."

I'm being replaced by another girl whose name starts with A. I'm not sure why that makes it even worse, but it does. First Allen got my proposal and now Amy is getting my apartment. I can't tell if I'm about to break down into tears or go into a mindless rage and upend the table on Parker. Probably both, especially as his words sink in.

"How long have you been seeing her?" I ask.

Parker ducks his head, like he expects me to throw something at it. "About two months now."

"Two. Months." My whole world has turned upside down.

All this time I've been mentally planning our wedding while he's been banging some other woman.

"It just happened. A dumb work fling, but then it turned into more. I'm sorry."

"You're sorry?" My voice is veering into screeching territory and I don't give a single fuck. "You've been cheating on me for two whole months and you're kicking me out of our apartment and you're *sorry?*"

Parker glances around at the other diners, who are all staring at us. "Keep your voice down. Like I said, I never meant to hurt you, but I really need you out of my place by the end of the week."

The absolute nerve of him. He knows how much this screws me over. I'm so upset I can't even form words. Instead, I grab my wine and toss it in his face. For a second I savor his look of shocked horror that probably mirrors my own, and then I turn on my heel and storm out of the restaurant.

On the sidewalk two men are kissing, one in an expensive charcoal suit, the other in a beige delivery uniform. They break apart as I walk by, beaming at each other, and I catch the name *Allen* on the front of the uniform.

"Congrats," I tell them, smiling through my tears. At least one of us is having a good day.

CHAPTER TWO

ALLIE

ONCE I REGAIN control of myself—which involves hiding in the bathroom of a drugstore until I finish ugly crying, then spending another five minutes fixing my makeup while cursing Parker's name—I text my best friend Brooke and ask her to meet me.

"I can't believe him," Brooke says, twenty minutes later. I'm lucky I was near the law firm where she works and that she was able to meet me at a nearby coffee shop. She listened to my entire sob story while rage made her dark blue eyes look black. "That scumbag. I knew he wasn't good enough for you."

I fold my arms on the table and bury my face in them with a groan. My eyes are all dry and scratchy from crying and my heart aches. "Two months. Two. Freaking. Months."

Brooke rubs my back in slow circles. "I'm going to murder him. Or at least sue his ass for all he's worth."

"I thought he was going to propose! I can't believe I was such an idiot."

"You're not an idiot, but you should get a blood test. You don't know how many people he stuck his dick in."

I sit up with a groan. "Is that supposed to make me feel better?"

"Sorry, I'm no good at this touchy-feely emotional stuff. But if you want realistic advice, I'm your girl." She hands me a tissue from her black Coach purse. Brooke's style is minimalistic chic, and she never wears any color other than black and white. The one exception is her nails, which she always paints in a dramatic color. Today they're a deep, luxurious purple.

If we were in a movie, Brooke would be the gorgeous, workaholic heroine and I'd be her curvy, funny friend. But this isn't a movie, and there's no Hollywood ending for either of us in sight.

I wipe my face and blow my nose. "You can help by finding me a place to live. Parker said he wants me out by the end of the week."

Brooke scoffs. "He can't do that."

"He can. Thanks to my stupidity I gave up my own apartment to move in with him and my name isn't on the lease. I have nowhere to go, and since I'm on summer break, I'm too broke to afford a deposit on a new place. I'm screwed."

"You can stay with me."

"No thanks. Your place is so tiny I'm not sure it actually qualifies as an apartment. We'd murder each other after a week." Her miniscule studio near her office costs a fortune anyway—one of the downsides of living in Los Angeles. Hence my dilemma. Anything I can afford on my tiny salary will be so far away from the private high school in Santa Monica where I teach that I'll spend my entire life in traffic. Assuming I could somehow scrape together enough cash for a deposit plus first and last month's rent, which seems unlikely.

She lifts one shoulder. "It's better than nothing."

I scrunch my nose up. "Is it though?"

She tucks a strand of golden blond hair back into her tight bun. "Fine. What about your sister? Surely you can move in with her."

I practically choke on my green tea. "No way. I'd never hear the end of it. Kristen would gloat forever about how her silly baby sister went and did some stupid thing again and needed her big sister to bail her out. Again. I can't do that."

Brooke taps her purple nails on the side off her coffee cup. "Hmm. I might have a solution for you, but it's not ideal."

"What is it? I'll take just about anything at this point."

"My brother has an empty guest room in his house in Malibu and he owes me a favor."

My eyebrows shoot up. "The actor? You said he was a 'cocky prick.' Your words, not mine."

"He is. But you know what he's not? A random stranger from the internet who might end up making a suit out of your skin. Plus his house is big, and he's ridiculously anal, so it'll be clean at least. You'd just have to put up with the royal ass until you're back on your feet again."

I swirl my tea around in my cup as I consider. "I don't really have any other options."

Brooke types away on her phone. "I'm texting him now about it."

"Thanks. You're a lifesaver."

"You won't thank me when he makes you cry on a daily basis. You sure you don't want to ask your sister for help?"

"Very sure."

"Fine, but don't say I didn't warn you." She points her phone at me. "And whatever you do, don't get a crush on him."

I let out a miserable laugh. "That's definitely not in the cards."

"Really? Because I know you. You meet a halfway decent guy. You fall instantly head over heels in love and start seeing babies and dogs and a minivan. You make reckless decisions like moving in with him way too soon. Sound familiar?"

"It wasn't reckless..." I say, even though everything she said was spot on.

"You're a romantic. It's one of your most endearing qualities, but it means you need to be careful too. My brother's single and he's not a bad looking guy. Until he opens his mouth and ruins it with his personality, anyway."

"You don't need to worry. I am done with love. Totally over it. As far as I'm concerned, romance can suck a big one. Besides, I've seen your brother on TV before. He's not my type." Okay, that's not entirely true. Shane Easton is a damn fox, but he's probably Photoshopped or wearing tons of makeup or whatever they do to make actors look hot all the time, even when they're sweaty and tired. In person there's no way he actually looks like that. "If he's half as bad as you say he is, I won't be interested anyway."

"Uh huh," she says. "Shane says he can meet you tonight at five. That work?"

"Perfect." That gives me enough time to run back to the apartment and pack my things.

"Don't get any ideas about the other roommates either. They're all actors and—" She pauses and glances down at her phone, which is vibrating. "Shit, I have to run. I have a meeting with a client that I can't miss." She downs her coffee in one gulp, grabs her purse and jumps to her feet, only stopping to give me a quick hug. "I'll text you Shane's address. Everything is going to be fine, I promise."

After she speeds out, I finish my tea and sit up a little straighter, bolstered by her words. My love life may be in shambles, and I may have no place to live and only a few pennies to my name, but at least I have the best friend in the world.

Her brother and his roommates can't be that bad...right?

CHAPTER THREE

ALLIE

THIS CAN'T BE the place.

I switch off my car and stare at the house in front of me. Actually, house is an understatement. Something this gigantic and majestic can only be called a mansion. Or a beach house, considering the glimpse of the bright blue ocean behind it.

A really freaking *huge* beach house.

I check the address on my phone. Then the numbers on the house. Then my phone again. The numbers. My phone. The house. It all checks out, but my brain can't seem to connect the dots.

I text Brooke just in case. *Are you sure this is the right place?*

Yep. Told you it was big.

Big? No. Not even close. This? Is freaking massive. And completely unbelievable.

It's like I've stumbled onto the set of *The Bachelor* and at any moment some guy in a tux is going to hand me a rose.

Except I don't have a limo to get out of, just my old Ford Focus with no less than three warning lights on the dashboard.

As I swing my leg out, green tea in hand, I'm gaping at the house so much that my kitten heel catches on the edge of the door and I stumble. I recover quickly, but not before spilling tea down the front of my dress.

Classy, that's me all right.

I quickly grab some napkins from the glove box of my car and try to clean myself off. This dress is one of my favorites—mint green with white polka dots, tight in the bodice and flared at the waist, the epitome of retro cute—and I'll hate myself forever if I've ruined it. I do the best I can to clean it up, then ball up the napkins and toss them in my car. I don't think the dress will stain, but the wet fabric clings to my body in ways that leave little to the imagination. Not exactly the best way to make an impression.

While it dries, I lean against the side of my car and take stock of my surroundings. The house looks like an architect's wet dream, with square arches, huge windows, and hard edges. Everything is stark white mixed with metal and glass. Palm trees and ferns soften the ultra-modern exterior, as does the nearby lapping of waves and the cool ocean breeze. A huge fence surrounds the property, and as I stand there, the gate closes, trapping me inside.

There's no way this can be the right place. If it is, I definitely don't belong here. I certainly couldn't afford a room in that house, not on my measly salary. But I came all this way, through the windy roads of Malibu, and I might as well go inside. What other option do I have?

I step up to the door, smooth my wayward red hair, and ring the doorbell. A soft chime sounds within. Through the glass, I can see all the way through the house to the sparkling ocean on the other side. Beachfront property. In Southern California. This place must have cost a fortune.

A guy opens the door and my heart skips a beat because he's definitely the most beautiful guy I've ever seen in person before. I'm not even exaggerating, he looks like an actual underwear model, the kind you only see in black and white and wearing Calvin Klein briefs. He's got lush, dark brown hair with a hint of curl that's effortlessly messy but probably took him hours to perfect, and his hazel eyes have a mischievous glint to them. There's something familiar about him too, although I can't place him.

A sexy grin spreads across his face. "You must be Allison. Come on in."

I swallow back that awkwardness that comes from meeting someone so good looking and step inside. "Thanks."

"I'm Matt. Nice to meet you. Brooke never mentioned her best friend was so gorgeous." He offers me his hand, except when I move to shake it, he bends to kiss my knuckles like some hero from a historical romance novel. The move is so unexpected and cheesy that I burst out laughing.

"Please, call me Allie," I tell him with a smile. This one's a flirt, that's for sure. I'm surprised Brooke didn't warn me away from him instead of her brother.

"Welcome, Allie," a smooth voice says behind me.

I turn toward the sound, and now I'm really tongue-tied because this guy is not only ridiculously handsome, but he's famous too. Like, super famous. Followed by paparazzi hoping for a shirtless photo famous. Dated Taylor Swift and had a song written about the breakup famous. Named People's Sexiest Man Alive this year famous.

"Hi," I manage to get out, though it sounds more like a squeak. Hey, I'm not shy. I teach high school kids, after all. But holy crap, I'm standing in front of Luke Hart. Even I can get totally star-struck. It's never happened to me before, but I've also never been in a celebrity beach house before. Not to mention, his face is the epitome of masculine perfection and his body is seriously a piece of art. He's ridiculously buff, befitting a guy who plays action heroes in movies. I'm pretty sure his arms are bigger than my thighs and my thighs are not small, trust me on that.

That explains why Matt looks familiar. He's Luke Hart's younger brother, with the same sexy tousled dark brown hair and hazel eyes, and he's also an actor, although not nearly as famous. He's been in a couple of his brother's movies in small roles, plus he was on a TV show that only lasted one season, but I can't recall anything he's done since.

Luke holds out his hand and I stare at it for way too long before shaking it. I really need to get it together, but how? I've seen this guy naked before. Not in person of course, but on a giant movie screen, which might be even worse. Now all I can think about is how big he is.

Literally.

"I'm Luke Hart, but you probably knew that already." He flashes me an amused smile, like he's entertained by how nervous and awkward I am. He must get this all the time. "You met my brother already. And that guy over there is Shane Easton."

With all the eye candy on display, I didn't even notice the other man in the room, even though he's the one I was expecting to meet today. Brooke's brother stands at the floor-to-ceiling window across from us, gazing out at the ocean. Even from behind, he's an exquisite specimen of masculinity, with broad shoulders, a muscular back, and a perfect ass I try really hard not to stare at. But who am I kidding? I totally stare.

Shane turns toward us slowly with the setting sun behind him, highlighting his profile. My breath catches and I pray he's not as devastatingly handsome as he is on TV, but no, it's even worse, because he's somehow even better looking in person.

The light catches his dark blonde hair and turns it to pure gold. My eyes linger over everything from his straight nose to his high cheekbones to his defined jaw with the perfect amount of five 'o'clock shadow. His muscled abs are visible through his thin black t-shirt, and the sleeves end in exactly the right spot to show off his strong arms. He towers over me, looking every inch the sexy, brooding superhero he plays on TV, and my already racing heart threatens to run away from me entirely.

I try to regain my composure, reminding myself that he's Brooke's brother and even though she said he's a jerk, he's doing me a huge favor. This is going to work out and everything will be fine.

I step forward and flash him a big smile, optimism radiating from my pores, then hold out my hand to him. "Hi, I'm Allie Chambers. Thanks for letting me stay with you for a while."

His eyes, the color of the darkest ocean depths, slowly examine me from head to toe and a scowl spreads across his gorgeous mouth, like he's offended by what he sees. Maybe it's my dress, which is still damp from the tea I spilled on it, or maybe it's my short, extra curvy body filling it. He probably only dates tall, skinny actresses in designer clothes and I'm the complete opposite of that. As his haughty stare fixes on my face again, I hold my hand out another few seconds, embarrassment creeping up the back of my neck.

"You're Brooke's friend?" he asks, his voice dripping with disdain.

What. A. Dick.

I finally drop my hand. "Yes, I am."

His frown deepens and he pointedly looks away. I want to sink into the marble floor and disappear. It's black and white and beautiful in a cold, stark way, like everything else in this living room, including the man in front of me. My green dress is the brightest thing here. I'm a scoop of mint ice cream that's fallen off its cone and is melting on the sidewalk.

I'm tempted to run out of the house, hop in my car, and speed away while praying I never see any of these guys again, but I'm tired of letting men step all over me and more than a little desperate too. Shane might think he can dissuade me from staying here with his complete lack of manners, but he's nothing compared to the sixteen-year-old boys I deal with on a daily basis. I can handle him.

"It's nice to meet all of you." I prop my hands on my hips, slap on a confident smile, and face the three people I'm going to be living with for the next few months. Three of the sexiest men in Hollywood…who happen to be my new roommates.

CHAPTER FOUR

SHANE

BROOKE'S FRIEND is fucking gorgeous.

There is absolutely no way she can move in with us.

The second I saw her, it was like every part of me woke from a long sleep. She stirred something deep inside me with her bright smile, wavy red hair, and that retro dress that hugged her curves. And those curves, damn. A man could lose himself in a body like that for days and never want to come up for air. I tried to look away, to make the tightening in my chest and in my jeans stop, but by then it was already too late. The damage was done.

I saw the way the other guys checked her out too. Matt, like she was going to be his next one night stand. Luke, like she was another fangirl he'd fuck to forget his ex-wife. I can't let either of those things happen. Not to my sister's best friend.

"Why don't you tell us a little about yourself?" Matt asks, sliding an arm around Allie's shoulders. He leads her to one of the boxy white sofas in the living room, while casually stroking her back.

She sits beside him with a friendly smile and then launches into a long spiel without once stopping for air. "Well, I'm a high school English teacher, although I'm on summer break right now, so I'm only teaching a few hours of summer school. I have an older sister named Kristen who is a vet. Brooke and I were college roommates and we've been best friends ever since. I'm deathly afraid of spiders. I like to bake and craft and read. I love holidays, every single one of them. And anything that's colorful and sparkly. Oh, and animals. Dogs, cats, birds, you name it, I love them all."

"No pets," I snap.

"No pets, got it." She flashes me a smile, but it's different from the one she gave Matt. This one says, *bite me*. It also shows off the dimples in her cheeks, which somehow manage to be both cute and sexy at the same time.

"What happened to your last place?" Luke asks, from where he's perched on the arm of the couch.

Her smile falls. "My boyfriend dumped me and kicked me out of our apartment. I thought he was proposing. There was this plane and these flowers and—oh, never mind. Turns out he'd been cheating on me for two months." She lets out a pitiful laugh, then quickly looks at me, her green eyes turning hard again as they meet mine. "Brooke said you have a spare room I can use for a while. I'll pay whatever I can and after school starts again I'll be able to save up some money for a new place."

Shit, this keeps getting worse. Not only is she a beautiful woman in a house full of single guys who are used to getting any girl they want, but she just got out of a serious relationship. She's like a mouse caught between three cats, all sharpening their claws and eyeing her with hunger. Any one of us could pounce on her.

Not that I would, of course. I have no interest in her. Seriously.

"We need to discuss this," I say, glancing at Luke and Matt. "Privately."

The guys both flash Allie their trademark charming smiles, then follow me into my office at a leisurely pace. I shut the door behind us and turn to them. "This isn't going to work."

"What's the problem?" Matt asks.

Luke leans against the edge of my desk. "I like her. It was cute how flustered she got around us."

I give them both a level glare. "She's a woman."

Matt grins. "Glad you noticed. I was starting to think you'd forgotten what that was."

I cross my arms, ignoring his jab. "One woman living with three men. You don't see a problem there?"

Matt shrugs. "It's only temporary."

Luke rubs his chin as he considers. "There are definitely pros and cons to living with a woman. Pro, she's really hot. Con, we can't walk around in only our underwear anymore."

"I don't see why not." A slow grin spreads across Matt's face. "Maybe she'd join us."

"No, she won't," I say. Why am I the only one who sees what a disaster this is going to be? With three cocky guys like us in one house, it's a miracle we all get along as we do. Adding a woman into the mix will only complicate things. Especially one who we're all picturing in her underwear at this very moment.

"She has nowhere else to go," Matt says. "I vote she can stay."

"Me too," his older brother adds.

My jaw clenches. "Too bad neither of you gets a vote. This is my house, not a damn democracy."

Matt rolls his eyes. "Fine, we don't get a vote, but we can tell you when you're being a dick. Like now."

"You took me in when I had nowhere else to go, and we should do the same for her," Luke says.

Matt nods. "If nothing else, do it because your sister is going to bust your balls if you don't."

Dammit. As much as I hate it, they're both right. I owe Brooke a big favor, and if I let her best friend stay here for a few months, then we'll be even. It's not like we don't have the space in the house for Allie either. I can't exactly say no. Especially when she has nowhere else to go.

But this? This can only end badly.

"Fine. I'll let her stay on one condition," I tell them. "We all have to swear not to sleep with her."

Matt blinks at me. "Seriously?"

"I saw the way you two checked her out. You can't tell me you weren't thinking about fucking her."

"Us?" he asks. "What about you?"

"There is zero chance of that happening."

Luke shrugs. "It's a damn shame, but I'll agree if you two do."

Matt gives a dramatic sigh. "Fine."

"I want it in writing too," I add.

"Of course you do," Matt says, rolling his eyes again.

With that settled, I throw open the door and walk back into the living room. Allie's moved to the window to look out at the view of the ocean, and she turns toward us as we approach. The split second of nervous vulnerability on her face makes my chest tighten again, but then it's gone, replaced by her determined eyes and a big smile.

"Everything okay?" she asks.

The other guys look to me, and I force out the words, "We've decided you can stay."

Relief softens her features and she moves forward like she's about to hug me, but restrains herself at the last second. Barely. "Thank you. I can't afford much, but I'll pay you whatever I can."

"I don't want your money," I say, disgusted by the very idea.

That only makes her stand taller. "Then I'll do whatever I can to make it up to you. I'll cook, I'll clean, I'll do laundry. Whatever you need."

"We have people who handle all that."

Her eyes widen. "Oh. Right. But—"

Luke rests a hand on her arm. "You're not a servant. You're our guest. Relax and enjoy your summer break."

"We'll take good care of you," Matt says, and I shoot him a harsh glare.

"Okay," Allie says, with a genuine smile for the two of them. "But you better believe I'm still going to bake for you."

"I can't wait," Luke says, even though his personal trainer would murder him if he so much as looked at a baked good.

"I'll show you to your room," I say, before the other guys can charm her into their beds.

I quickly debate which room to give her. The house is three stories, descending down the cliff toward the beach, and the three of us live on separate floors. I'm loathe to share my floor with anyone else, but I can't stick her next to Matt either. Even if he doesn't seduce her, she'll have to put up with his revolving door of women every night. No, better to keep her close so I can keep an eye on her and make sure they both stay out of trouble.

I head down the stairs without waiting to see if she will follow. A few seconds later, her footsteps sound behind me. "Luke is on the top floor with the living room and kitchen," I tell her as we hit the second floor. "Matt is on this level, along with the gym and theater. You'll be on the lowest floor with me."

"This place is amazing," she says, and I feel a touch of pride at the awe in her voice.

We hit the lower level and I head directly to her room. It's the smallest bedroom in the house, but it makes up for it with a walk-in closet, floor-to-ceiling windows, and direct access to the pool and the beach. The previous owners used it as a nursery, but I converted it to a guest room, though no one has stayed in it before.

"Wow," she says, as she steps into the room. "It's so…"

I wait for her to say something like "impressive" or "stunning." Compared to what she's probably used to, this room must be a big step up.

"Bland," she finishes.

"Bland," I repeat.

"White walls. White sheets. White furniture. No art. No knickknacks." She sounds horrified, but then she draws in a breath. "That's okay. Nothing that a little decorating and a fresh coat of paint won't fix."

My eyes narrow. "No paint."

She looks like she might argue, but then she nods. "How soon can I move in?"

"As soon as you want."

"Thank you. I really do appreciate this so much. This room is perfect." Her clear green eyes gaze up at me and she gives me a genuine smile. "If it weren't for you, I don't know what I would do. Live out of my car, probably."

Her words make me temporarily speechless, and as I stare at her soft lips I'm hit with the strongest urge to kiss her. Or throw her on the bed and show her how not bland this room would be with her naked skin and red hair against those white sheets.

This is unacceptable. Allie is a complication and that's the last thing I need right now. I have enough complications at work thanks to an ill-fated relationship with my co-star. I don't need them in my home too.

I thrust the keys at her. "Don't get too comfortable. This is only temporary."

I can't prevent her from moving in. I can't kick her out. But I can do everything in my power to get her to leave.

CHAPTER FIVE

ALLIE

YOU WERE RIGHT, I text Brooke. *Your brother is a jerk.*
Told you, Brook replied. *Ready to move in with me yet?*
Nope. This place is worth the hassle.
Good luck with that.

I gaze across my new bedroom. Even though there's barely anything in here, I'll make it work. It's a blank canvas, ready for me to splash myself all over it. It's a good size and has a walk-in closet and large windows overlooking the ocean. There's even a door that leads outside to the pool. The bathroom isn't attached but is right next door, which is fine. It's as empty, white, and unused as the bedroom is.

I take the stairs back to the top floor, which is an open concept design with the living room, dining room, and kitchen all flowing together in one big space. Everything in the house is sparsely decorated, but of the finest quality. There's no color other than black, white, and gray, along with a lot of metal and glass. Even the floors are white and pristine. Shane and his sister share the same style preferences, it seems.

I find Matt in the kitchen, pouring himself a glass of water. For a moment all I can do is stare at him and marvel at how I'm going to be living with three incredibly sexy guys for the next few months. If I needed a way to get over Parker fast, this is definitely a good start.

"Did Shane give you the run-down of the place?" Matt asks.

"Not exactly."

He rolls his eyes. "Of course not. The main thing to know is that Shane likes things done his way and he can't stand mess or disorder."

I hold up my hands. "Not a problem. He won't even know I'm here."

"And whatever you do, don't touch the thermostat."

My eyebrows dart up. "That sounds like a challenge."

He grins. "Trust me, you won't like the consequences."

"All right. I won't mess with it." I gesture to the front door. "I'm going to grab my stuff from the car."

"Need some help?"

"That'd be great, thanks."

We head outside, where my car waits under a palm tree, the scratched blue paint glinting under the sun. Like me, it's out of place here. I pop the hatchback trunk and grab as many bags as possible from inside, loading them up on my arms.

Matt picks up the two boxes in the back, his well-developed arms flexing as he lifts them easily. The boxes were heavy when I put them in, but that doesn't seem to be a problem for him. "That's it?"

I shrug, but glance away quickly. "I don't need much."

We carry everything down the stairs to my new bedroom. Once my things are all on the bed, it does seem pretty pitiful. I have more stuff at my old apartment, but the idea of facing Parker makes me think it's time to downsize anyway.

Matt lingers in the doorway, leaning against the frame in a way that draws my eyes to the t-shirt stretching against his muscles. The craziest thing is he seems to be checking me out too. Don't get me wrong, I'm pretty damn cute, especially if you're into a woman with some extra curves. But I figured most actors would go for the tall, thin model types, not girls like me. Not that I have a problem with tall, thin model types, mind you. All bodies are perfect, no matter their shape. I'm just a little self-conscious of mine sometimes, especially in a city like Los Angeles where looks matter so much.

"How about I give you a tour?" Matt asks.

"I'd love that."

He steps back into the hall and gestures at the door across from mine. "That's Shane's bedroom. I suggest you not go in there if you value your life."

"Not a problem."

He takes me to an open doorway down the hall. "This is where we hang out most of the time."

We step inside a family room that's a lot more relaxed than the living room upstairs, with large, gray couches, a table and chairs, and a huge TV. Tall windows let in a ton of light and sliding doors lead outside to a massive pool with an attached spa.

Matt leads me onto the patio and I breathe in the fresh sea air. The sun's still high in the sky, signaling a warm summer night to come, and all I want to do is strip off my clothes and jump in this pool. Preferably with Matt. It's one of those pools that seems to have no edge, making it appear as if it descends directly into the ocean. Beyond it, steps lead down to the beach, which is private and empty, a rarity in Southern California.

"Feel free to use the pool or the spa anytime you want," Matt says. "You can get to the beach from here too, but make sure you bring a key because the gate will lock behind you."

"This is incredible. Like something out of a movie. You know?" I laugh, because it's a ridiculous comment to make to an actor. "Of course you know."

"It is incredible," Matt says, with his sexy grin. "Come on, I'll show you the rest of the place."

As we head back inside to continue the tour, I ask something that's been nagging at me. "I hope this isn't too personal of a question, but why are three famous actors all living here? Couldn't you each get your own fancy beach houses like this one?"

His smile fades and he clears his throat. "I'm sort of in between gigs right now, so Shane lets me live here while I look for my next part. In the meantime, I work as a bartender nearby."

"And your brother?"

"He can easily afford a place like this, or even bigger, but he's laying low for a while. Did you hear about his divorce?"

"Of course." I know every gory detail about Luke's messy divorce from actress Lana Grayson earlier this year. Everyone does. It was all over every magazine and entertainment news show, with everyone on social media mourning the end of #luna. Luke and Lana met on the set of a movie three years ago and were both gorgeous, rich, and popular. Even their names sounded good together. They were the perfect couple, until Lana left Luke for the co-star of her last movie.

"Lana took the house," Matt says. "Or really, he let her

have it. He had nowhere to go and was kind of a mess at the time. Drinking. Drugs. Women. Shane told him to stay here as long as he needed to get his shit together again. That was four months ago."

"Sounds like Shane takes in all sorts of charity cases."

"I know he comes across as an asshole at first, but the truth is, he's a good guy. He wouldn't open his house up to three lost people otherwise."

"You sure? Maybe Shane needs rent money for his secret gambling problem."

Matt laughs. "No gambling problem. He definitely doesn't need the money, not with his show. In fact, he barely lets me pay him anything for rent. If it were up to him I'd live here for free, but I insist."

We make it to the middle floor to continue the tour of my temporary home. Matt shows me the gym, with enough equipment in it to give 24 Hour Fitness a run for its money. The home theater is next to it, with plush leather seats and a huge screen. We pass by another guest room that's bigger than mine, but doesn't have a view of the ocean or a walk-in closet. Shane could have easily stuck me in this room, but he didn't. He gave me the nicer room. The one near him.

Back on the first floor, Matt shows me a grocery list that they fill out each week, which Shane and Luke's assistants then take care of. He explains that the cleaning crew comes every Friday morning and that they also do laundry. A personal chef comes three times a week and on the other days healthy pre-prepared meals are delivered ready to heat up. "If you need anything dry cleaned, Shane's assistant will take care of that too," he adds.

I chew on my lower lip as I stare at the grocery list. "Wow.

I'm not sure I'm comfortable with all that. I'm used to taking care of myself."

Matt shrugs. "Suit yourself. But you might as well go with it. Shane's paying for it, after all."

I'm still unsure about the idea of letting someone else do all the cleaning, cooking, and shopping. What am I supposed to do with myself? I like cooking, after all. Maybe they'll let me take over some of the household duties in return for letting me stay with them. It will make me feel better for not being able to pay rent as well.

Matt continues his tour. "Down this hallway is Luke's room and Shane's office. I'd avoid both of those if I were you."

I laugh. "Will do."

"If you need anything, let me know." He grins at me and his eyes travel up and down my body suggestively. "Anything at all."

He's such a flirt. I can't deny that I like it though, maybe even a little too much. After what Parker did, it's nice to have a guy interested in me.

"Thanks you for your help. I'm going to go unpack." I lean forward and press a quick kiss to his cheek, before heading to the stairs.

CHAPTER SIX

ALLIE

ONCE I'M in my room, I stare at all my stuff. I don't have much. I gave up a lot of my furniture when I moved in with Parker, and my apartment before that was tiny anyway. Still, I was in such a rush to pack my belongings after our disastrous lunch that I left a lot of my things behind. Now I regret it.

A sharp knock sounds on my door. "Come in," I call out.

Shane steps inside, looking every bit as gorgeous as he did when I first saw him, even though his blue eyes are still like ice. "You seem to be settling in."

"Yep. Pretty much done unpacking."

He hands me a couple sheets of paper, stapled together. "Sign this."

I take them and skim the first page. A bunch of legal mumbo jumbo makes me nearly cross-eyed. "What is this?"

"Roommate contract." He hands me a black pen.

"I see." Except, as I read, it quickly becomes clear this isn't a normal rental agreement. The first page is a pretty standard non-disclosure agreement, which I suppose is to be expected when living with three famous people. I turn the page and my eyes widen. I begin to read out loud. "'I, Allison Chambers, agree not to engage in any sexual activities with anyone living in this house'—what the hell?"

"It's for your own good."

I glare at him. "What I do with my body is no concern of yours."

"What goes on in my house is a concern of mine, especially if it causes problems between the people living here." He offers the pen more insistently. "We're all going to sign a copy."

"And if I don't?"

"Then you can find somewhere else to live."

I continue reading, scowling the entire time. "'Sexual activities with anyone living in this house, including but not limited to kissing, intercourse, oral sex, handjobs, anal sex—'" My eyes widen. "Wow, who wrote this?"

"I did. Sign it or pack your bags."

I snatch the pen from his fingers. "Fine. But just so you know, I would never sleep with any of you anyway. The very idea is so arrogant, so ridiculous, so—"

"I'm not worried about you. I'm worried about them."

I huff. "I doubt they're even interested."

"They are. Any man would be." His eyes slowly rake up and down my body in a way that brings heat to my cheeks.

"Even you?"

His face goes blank again, his mouth twisting. "No. Not me."

Of course not. I scrawl my name across the bottom of his contract, then shove the papers at his chest. His very firm chest. "Anything else? Want me to get a permission slip every time I use the restroom? Or fill out a form when I want to bring a guy home with me?"

His eyes narrow. "You can bring home as many guys as you want. No form required."

I prop my hands on my hips. "Good! Because I'm going to bring *a lot* of men home with me! Dozens of them, in fact!"

"Fine!" He snatches the pen from my hand and storms out of the room before slamming the door to his bedroom, leaving me scowling at nothing.

I slam my own door, just because, then shove my things off the bed so I can collapse on top of it.

Now that I'm alone, the day catches up to me. I started this morning full of hope and happiness, with a sense that everything was going to be magical today. Then I had lunch with Parker and saw the plane and...well, we all know how that went.

After meeting with Brooke, I ran back to my apartment and shoved everything I could in my car through my tears, then raced over here. Now I've somehow found myself living with three of the sexiest men alive in a huge freaking beach house. How is this my life?

My phone buzzes and Brooke's name flashes on the screen. "What's up?" I ask.

"Just calling to see how you're doing," she says. "You're not a big crying mess, are you?"

I can't help but laugh. "Not at the moment, but the night's still young."

"Good. Are the guys treating you okay?"

"Yeah, they're fine." I sit up and stare out the window at my new ocean view. "Why didn't you tell me who they were though? Or about how amazing this place is? You could have prepared me better!"

"I didn't think it was that big a deal," she says.

"Not that big a deal? I'm living in a beach house with the hottest men in Hollywood!"

"Hmm, I suppose for a bunch of dudes they're attractive. I didn't think of that. Sorry."

I sigh. Brooke is a lesbian, so I can forgive her for her lack of foresight in this matter. Plus, her family is wealthy, so maybe this amazing house is normal to her too. Either way, she saved my butt when she convinced her brother to let me stay here, so I can't be upset with her.

"Just don't go falling for any of them," she says. "This is only temporary, remember."

"Of course. I have a firm 'look but don't touch' policy in place. Not to mention, your brother made us all sign this contract saying no sexy times are allowed between any of us." I grin to myself. "Besides, how would I choose between them?"

"Allie..."

I flop back on the bed. "I know, I know. Don't worry about me. I'm fine."

"Okay, good." She pauses and I hear shuffling in the background. "Hey, I have to go. I have a date tonight with a girl in Accounting."

"Ooh, have fun. Let me know how it goes."

"I will."

We hang up and I stare at the white ceiling overhead, trying to relax. Except as I lie there the breakup with Parker plays through my head again. I wasted one year on him and he betrayed me and tossed me aside like I was nothing. The worst part is I still care for him. I wanted to marry the guy, after all.

It'll take some time for me to get over him. I just pray it won't be too long. I don't want the asshole taking up any more of my life. I want to move on.

At least I have three sexy-as-sin guys to distract me from Parker—even if I'm not allowed to do anything with them. Whatever, I can still look. And fantasize about them from the privacy of my own room.

The best part is: in those fantasies, I don't have to choose only one.

CHAPTER SEVEN

ALLIE

I SPEND my first night in the beach house moping over my ex, but in the morning I decide to put Parker out of my thoughts for the rest of the day. Hell, the rest of my *life*. And as my way of thanking the guys for letting me live here with them, I head upstairs to make them some breakfast.

I step into the kitchen and marvel at how big and beautiful it is, like something out of a home design catalog. Everything is new and shiny and pristine. I begin opening cabinets, checking out what kind of cooking setup they have here. They have gorgeous cookware and quite a few ingredients stashed in the pantry, but they're missing a few things I'll need. Luckily I come prepared.

After a quick trip back to my room, I've spread everything I need across the kitchen counter and get to work. I don't know what the guys like, or if they're gluten-free or allergic to nuts or what, so I decide to make two of my favorite treats.

I sing to myself while I work and soon the kitchen smells like warmth and happiness. It's also completely covered in flour and chocolate chips and coconut, but hey, that's how it goes. I'll clean up later. Promise.

Footsteps sound behind me and I turn to see Luke emerging from his room. He's not wearing a shirt, just a pair of boxers hanging low on his well-defined hips, and my jaw falls open at the sight. It's impossible not to stare at his naked chest. He's the most ripped guy I've ever seen, like a Greek god come to life, with a fully developed six-pack and all sorts of definition on his chest that my eyes want to linger on. And the rest of me? It wants to trip and fall all over him in the hope he catches me, throws me over his shoulder, and carries me away like some kind of caveman.

Okay, Allie, those are seriously not feminist thoughts right there. But my body does not give a crap about any of that. It wants to be taken hard and fast on this kitchen counter, thank you very much.

I force myself to turn away from temptation. He's off-limits, as are the other guys in this house. Just because Parker and I were in a bit of a dry spell—and now I know why, that prick—and even before then things weren't that amazing between us in bed, doesn't mean I can jump on the first hot guy I see and dry hump his leg like a dog.

Even if he's really, really hot.

"Hey," Luke says, while opening the fridge. "Smells good in here."

"Thanks." I sneak another peek at his broad, sexy back as he grabs something, then shuts the door.

He leans against the counter next to me while he drinks a greenish smoothie that looks disgusting. His hair is perfectly tousled, his eyes lazy in a sultry way, like he just got out of bed after having the best sex of his life. "What are you making?"

"Pumpkin chocolate chip muffins and gluten-free coconut muffins."

"Those sound lovely, but we're all pretty strict about what we put in our bodies. I haven't had sugar in a year." He runs a hand over his hard stomach. "Takes a lot of work to stay in this kind of shape."

"Oh. Of course." I try not to sound disappointed. "What do you usually eat for breakfast?"

He raises his nasty-looking green smoothie. "Protein shake."

"Ew." I wrinkle my nose and he laughs. I've heard his laugh in movies before and in YouTube clips from interviews, but it's completely different in person somehow. Maybe because it's genuine. His presence seems to fill the room, his sheer charisma demanding my attention. It's no wonder he's the hottest movie star in the world right now.

Matt appears at the top of the stairs, blinking his eyes, looking adorably sleepy and sexy. He's wearing a shirt unfortunately, but underneath it—hot damn—he's only wearing tight black boxer briefs. They show off the whole very large package, and I'm pretty sure the temperature just went up in here by about ten degrees. I almost start to fan myself.

Are they purposefully taunting me with their forbidden hotness? Or do they always walk around like this?

Matt plucks a coconut muffin from the tray. "Ignore my brother. I will gladly eat your muffin." He flashes me a dirty smile. "And anything else you'd like to offer."

Luke snorts, then grabs one of the pumpkin muffins and throws it at his brother. Matt catches it in the air and takes a big bite out of it.

"Mmm...delicious," Matt says.

I shake my head, trying to hide my smile. "You two are trouble."

"The best kind," Luke says, with a wink, then turns to Matt. "You're up early today."

"Audition."

"Ah. Good luck."

A stern voice interrupts our fun. "What the hell is this?" Shane asks, standing at the top of the stairs and staring at the kitchen in horror. Unlike the others he's completely dressed, wearing black slacks and a white button-up shirt that somehow makes him just as sexy as the other two. "It looks like a bakery exploded in here."

"I made muffins," I say, my cheeks turning beet red.

"Did any of the ingredients actually make it into the muffins, or are they just all over the counters?"

I put my hands on my hips. "I was going to clean it up!"

"Don't listen to him, he's always cranky in the morning," Matt says. "Also these muffins are amazing, you should totally try one, Shane."

Shane gives Matt a withering look and storms off, toward his office. A door slams a few seconds later.

Luke shakes his head. "It's not the morning that makes him cranky, it's having to go to work with his ex."

"That would put anyone in a bad mood," I say, softening a little. I don't know much about what happened with his co-star Nadia, but last season on the TV show *Talon* their characters finally got together. If they aren't actually together in real life anymore I can see how that could make for an awkward work environment.

Which also gives me an idea.

While the other guys wander back to their rooms to

shower and get dressed, I pack up my muffins in two containers I find in a drawer. Then I march them over to Shane's office and knock on the door.

"Come in," he calls out.

I step inside, but am stunned speechless by the sight of the room. It's more of a library than an office, like something out of *Beauty and the Beast* with floor-to-ceiling shelves completely stuffed with books. There's even a reading nook in the corner. It makes my little English teacher heart thump faster and faster.

"What is it?" Shane asks, from where he sits at a desk.

"This room is incredible." I leave the muffins on his desk and practically skip over to the shelves. He has all sorts of different genres, from non-fiction to sci-fi and fantasy. There's also an entire shelf dedicated to books about the justice system.

He eyes the muffins I left in front of him. "What are these for?"

"To take with you on set today. Give them to the crew or your assistant or something." I shrug. "If you're this grumpy with them too they could probably use a nice gesture from you."

He stares at me with his mouth open for so long I fully expect another scolding, but then he reluctantly says, "That's not a bad idea. Thank you."

"You're welcome." I grin and decide to escape before he turns into a jerk again.

Allie 1, Shane 0.

CHAPTER EIGHT

MATT

WELL, that sucked.

Three hours of my life down the drain, and for what? For them to tell me they thought I should be more like my brother. Fuck that.

I'm not sure why I even bother anymore. My agent sends me scripts and gets me auditions, but no one wants me. They all want Luke, the big action star who graces the covers of magazines every month. I'm just the younger, crappier version of him.

When I get home, I grab a beer from the fridge and head to the den to lose myself in some video games before work. I find Allie sitting there still in her pajamas, her nose in a book with a half-naked guy on the cover. Her red hair is tied back in a lazy ponytail and the cutest reading glasses are perched on her little nose. Her pretty feet are curled up at her side, dotted with pink nail polish.

She glances up at me with a smile. "How did your audition go?"

For a second I'm too distracted by her casual sexiness, the kind she probably doesn't even realize she has. She's all lush curves and soft lips and warm eyes and I have the strongest urge to snuggle against her while we watch TV together. And maybe slide my hand into those pajama pants to touch her bare skin.

Problem is, I can't do either of those things. Thanks a lot, Shane.

I sigh and sit beside her, stretching my long legs out on the coffee table. "It didn't go well."

She sits up with a frown. "What happened?"

I shrug. "I wasn't what they were looking for, I guess."

"How is that possible?" She gestures at me. "I mean, look at you."

I raise an eyebrow at her. "What does that mean exactly?"

A slight pink flush touches her cheeks. "Oh, you know you're gorgeous. You could be an underwear model with that face and that body."

I grin at her compliment. Sure, I'm good-looking and plenty of women have told me so before, but it's different hearing her say it. Maybe because she's so genuine, or because she's not trying to get in my pants. "I have done a bit of modeling on the side. It pays the bills. But I really want to act." I take a sip of my beer. "Back to reading through scripts and hoping for a decent one."

"What was the part today?"

"A low budget action sci-fi movie. Like what my brother got started in. But they just wanted a copy of Luke."

"I'm sorry. I'm sure you'll find something that's a perfect fit soon."

"I wish I had your optimism."

Allie rests her hand on my arm, her touch soft. "It'll all work out. I'm sure of it. You just have to keep putting yourself out there and someone will see how special you are."

I chuckle. "That sounds like relationship advice."

"Oh, I'm definitely not giving you that. I'm no expert on relationships, obviously. That's how I ended up here, after all."

I take the hand that was on my arm and slowly run my thumb over her soft skin. "How are you doing with that?"

She sighs. "I'm fine. More mad at myself than anything."

"How could you possibly be mad at yourself?"

She glances away, as if embarrassed. "I should have noticed something was wrong. Should have seen the signs he was cheating on me. Looking back, there were definitely some hints, but I ignored them all. I told myself he was busy with work. Now I realize how stupid I was."

"Hey." I wrap an arm around her shoulders. "You are not stupid and none of this is your fault. Your ex was clearly the stupid one to cheat on you in the first place."

"Thanks. That's nice of you to say."

"I mean it. You're beautiful, kind, smart, and make amazing muffins. I've only known you a day and I can already tell a man would be a fool to give you up."

She gives me a shy smile. "Well, your flirting is definitely good for my ego."

I stare at her lips with the strongest urge to kiss her. From the way she gazes back at me I think she wants that too. There's an electricity in the air between us, and with her in my arms the draw to her mouth is so overwhelming it takes everything in my power to resist.

"Then my job here is done." I wink at her, then pull away.

"All right, I need to get ready for work. I'll let you get back to your book."

I actually have plenty of time, but I need to get away from her or I'll be tempted to tear up Shane's roommate contract, push her down on this couch, and go down on her until she stops thinking about her ex. That's what she needs—someone to make her forget that asshole and give her some confidence again. Someone to make her feel good.

That's my specialty.

I pause at the door. "You should come to the bar where I work tonight. Bring Brooke if you want. It'll be fun."

She bites her lip. "I'm not sure I'm ready."

"What else are you going to do? Mope around in your pajamas and watch cheesy movies?"

"Pretty much, yeah," she says, with a sad laugh.

"You've been doing that all day. Getting out will be good for you."

"I don't know..."

"Come to the bar and I'll make you the best drink you've ever had. When the guys fall all over you, you'll thank me. Trust me on this."

"Okay. Maybe. I'll think about it."

"Good."

I head back to my room, but as I change my clothes all I can think about is Allie. She's like those muffins she baked us this morning: warm, soft, and sweet. I bet she tastes just as delicious too. She's normally not my type at all, but there's something about her I can't stop thinking about.

I blame Shane. By making Allie forbidden, she became ten times hotter. I want to fuck her to get her out of my system, but that isn't going to happen. I probably just need to get laid. It has been a while. Like a week, maybe? Hey, that's a long time for me. But it's not a problem. I'm sure some girl at the bar tonight will be happy to take care of me.

Except the idea of sleeping with some random girl tonight no longer sounds appealing. There's only one woman I want to get in bed, and she's off-limits.

CHAPTER NINE

ALLIE

WHY OH WHY did I let Matt convince me to go out tonight?

I'm so not ready to move on. I told myself I was, but damn, breakups are *hard*. I'm still going through all those stages of grief over Parker, like anger and denial, and I'm not even close to acceptance yet. Even though I shouldn't waste a single minute thinking about him, he still finds his way back into my thoughts anyway. Being with someone for a year, living with them, and thinking you were going to get married will do that to you, I guess.

Going to the bar where Matt works seemed like a good way to stop the endless cycle of *why, why, why?* that was going through my head. Now I'm starting to think I made a big mistake.

The only saving grace is that this place is gorgeous. Sea Spray Lounge is an open-air bar resting right on the beach, up against the ocean. You can either sit at the covered bar, looking out at the water as the sun sets over it while the cool breeze brushes against your face, or walk out onto the patio where waves crash against the see-through barrier, which is lit with soft blue LED lights. More fairy lights dance along the top of the dark bar, giving the place a magical feel.

It's definitely more upscale than I imagined when Matt said I should head to a bar with him to pick up guys. People in here have money or are hoping to land someone with money, which I probably should have realized since we're in Malibu, after all.

The bar's fairly empty tonight and I take a stool at the counter right in front of Matt. Brooke couldn't make it and I feel awkward being here by myself. I've never been good at picking up guys in a bar, and despite what Matt said, guys don't usually hit on me either. I'm cute, but a lot of guys in LA aren't into women like me. Normally it doesn't bother me—I tell myself they can't handle these curves anyway—but now it reminds me that I'm alone and unwanted.

Geez, someone needs to slap the emo out of me already.

I distract myself by checking out Matt, who looks especially handsome in a black button-up shirt that's open at the neck to show off a hint of skin, just enough to make my mouth water. His sleeves are rolled up too, revealing his masculine wrists and forearms.

He leans on the bar in front of me with a sultry smile. "What'll it be, gorgeous?"

"Surprise me."

"Hmm." He tilts his head and a piece of wavy hair falls in front of his right eye. I have the strongest urge to tuck it back. "I'm guessing you're the kind of girl who likes fruity cocktails. The girlier the better."

I laugh. "Yep, that's me."

"Coming right up."

He turns around to prepare my drink and I check out his very nice ass in his black jeans. Then I scold myself in my head. I should not be checking out my roommates, no matter how hot they are.

A guy in a gray suit slides onto the barstool next to me. "Hey there. Can I get you a drink?"

I freeze up. This is why I'm here, isn't it? To forget Parker with some new guy. But all I can do is blink at this man while opening and closing my mouth like some kind of idiot.

He's good-looking, though not nearly as drop dead sexy as any one of my three roommates, but on an equal level with Parker. Before meeting Matt, Shane, and Luke, I'd have been all over this guy. Now he seems...ordinary.

That isn't the problem though. The problem is the fear that stuns me into silence, that whispers in the back of my mind *this guy will hurt you too.*

I can't do it. I can't.

Suddenly there's a large, comforting presence at my back. "She's with me."

The guy in the suit stares at the man behind me with wide eyes. Then he scrambles out of his seat, practically falling all over himself to move. "I'm so sorry, man. I didn't realize. I loved your last movie by the way."

"Thanks," Luke says.

As the guy runs off with his tail between his legs, Luke takes his place. I gape at him, much the same way I did the last guy, except this time I find my voice. "What was that?"

He shrugs, his voice smooth as he says, "I could tell you were uncomfortable."

"I would have handled it," I say, even though I'm secretly grateful I didn't have to.

"And now you can relax instead." He wears a black baseball cap pulled low that does a terrible job of hiding who he is. He'd need a full Darth Vader costume to stop people from recognizing him.

Matt returns with a pink drink in a martini glass with a rim covered in sugar. "Enjoy."

"What's this?" I ask. The drink is so pretty I want to snap a photo of it and put it on Instagram.

"Strawberry limoncello martini. It's my own specialty."

Luke snorts. "That's the drink he gives women to get them in bed with him. Watch out."

"No, that's the Screaming Orgasm." Matt winks at me. "I can give you one of those later though."

I shake my head with a smile as I grab the drink. It's a little sweet and a little sour and absolutely perfect. "Wow, this is amazing."

"I knew you'd like it." He slides a whiskey over to Luke, without even asking what he wants, and Luke nods in thanks. Matt then heads to the other end of the bar, where a woman in a red dress is waving him over.

"So let me guess," Luke drawls, as he sips his whiskey and eyes me. "My brother told you to come here tonight and find a guy to help you forget about your ex and now you're regretting listening to him."

"Yep, that about sums it up." I take another sip of my divine drink. Matt may be struggling as an actor, but he is definitely an incredibly talented bartender. And with his looks and charm, I bet he's never hurting for tips either.

"That's exactly the kind of thing Matt would tell you to do. And trust me, I tried his way too after Lana."

Lana. His ex, the famous actress. My eyes widen at the mention of her. I'm surprised he's bringing her up at all.

"But sleeping around never helped," Luke continues, staring into his whiskey. "Neither did the drinking."

"What did help?" I ask.

"Time and distance. That's about it." He rests an elbow on the bar, gazing into my eyes. "You've been betrayed by the person you loved. That's a terrible thing for anyone to go through. Cut yourself some slack and allow yourself to be sad about it. And if you can, try to get closure."

I'm not sure how to do that. Parker kicked me out, after all. "Did you ever get closure?"

His face darkens and he looks away. "I did. When we signed the divorce papers. That's when I was finally over her for good."

"I'm sorry. That must have been tough for you. Especially since it was so public."

"I won't lie, it's been a rough year. I can't go into the store without seeing my ex's face everywhere, or go online without hearing about her new movie. Leaving the country to film a movie helped. Staying off the internet did too. But that's part of being an actor and living in the spotlight. Everyone knows all of your business, or thinks they do anyway." He drains the whiskey and slams it down on the bar.

"I can't imagine how hard it must be to live in the spotlight all the time like that."

"Don't get me wrong, being an actor has its perks too. I signed up for this life and I'm not complaining. It's just that when shit hits the fan, everyone wants to take photos of it." He gives me a devastatingly handsome smile. "But I got through it, and you will too."

His words and his smile begin to unravel the knot of anxiety inside me. "Thanks for talking to me about all this. It helps."

"I'm glad." He rests his large hand over mine on the counter. "And remember, you're not in this alone. Even though you only moved in yesterday, we're here for you. All three of us."

"I appreciate that. Although I don't think Shane particularly wants me in his house."

"He does. A little too much, maybe." He leans forward, so his lips are almost brushing mine. "We all do."

With that, he slides off the barstool and walks outside to the patio, leaving me speechless.

CHAPTER TEN

ALLIE

AS I SETTLE in to the house and get used to living there, the guy's aren't around much over the next few days. They're all busy with their own lives and I see their assistants and staff members more than I see them. Shane is filming his TV show, spending long hours on set and coming home exhausted and cranky. Matt spends his nights at the bar and his days either sleeping or auditioning. Luke has to fly to London for reshoots of his movie at a moment's notice and we have no idea when he'll get back.

The peaceful solitude of the house is good for me though. It gives me time to get over Parker, which I've done by taping a giant picture of his face to my wall and throwing darts at it. After three days, I've gotten pretty good at hitting him right between the eyes. It's oddly therapeutic, although I cringe to think what Shane will say when he sees the little holes in his wall.

It helps that the house is truly an amazing place to live too. Every night as I fall asleep I can hear the waves gently lapping at the shore. In the morning, the crisp fog over the water is the perfect thing to wake up to. And in the evening, the sunsets are truly inspiring.

Not to mention, all the amenities of this place blow me away. In the theater I can watch movies for hours and it's like being at an actual cinema. The humongous kitchen is to die for, and the beach access and giant pool are unbelievable. My favorite thing is to sit outside under an umbrella, reading a romance novel and breathing in the ocean air. It's going to be hard to give this place up once I start teaching again and find my own apartment.

Since I'm on summer break I don't have much work to do, besides a few hours of summer school, but my sister Kristen asks me to help out at her veterinary office since her normal receptionist is on vacation for two weeks. It's decent money and the best part is I get to hang out with all the animals, although it breaks my heart when they come in sick or injured. I don't know how Kristen does it. Of course, playing with puppies and kittens does make up for some of the sad stuff.

However, working with my completely put-together older sister can sometimes be challenging, even though I love her a lot. She just makes me feel like a hot mess in comparison to her perfect self. And I don't think she even does it intentionally. Most of the time, anyway.

I'm glad for the work though because it allows me to start saving up some cash. I'll need it to get my own place soon. I can't keep relying on the hospitality of Shane and the other guys to let me live rent-free forever. Even if I have no desire to move out.

When I get home from a particularly crazy day at the vet's, I'm completely covered in cat hair. I head for the shower in the bathroom next to my room, but run straight into Shane's completely naked chest as he walks out of it. He's all wet and gorgeous and wearing only a towel and all I can do is stare at his muscles and broad shoulders and sculpted arms. He runs a hand across his chest idly and that only makes me stare even harder. I want to trail my fingers—or my tongue—all over him. Like those defined abs. Or those strong arms. Or the faint trail of hair leading down into the towel. Yum.

"Hi," I manage to say, and then suddenly I can't stop. "I just got back from working at my sister's office. She's a vet. I think I mentioned that. Anyway, I really need a shower because I'm totally allergic to cats, even though I love them. I actually have a cat tattoo on my ankle, which I got when I was drunk even though Brooke told me not to do it. Sometimes I think about getting it lasered off, but I kind of like it too." I cringe at my own words. I really should not be telling him this, but the sight of his almost-naked body has turned me into some kind of babbling moron. Worse, I can't stop staring. Like maybe if I stare hard enough my eyes will gain X-ray vision and I'll see through that towel.

"None of that surprises me." His eyes flicker down to my ankle and then slowly slide back up to my face. "The plumber is coming tomorrow. Until then, I'll be sharing this bathroom with you."

"Okay. Not a problem. It's your house after all." I giggle. Actually giggle. Like a silly girl who has lost her damn mind.

He gives me a long, even look, then turns around and goes back into his room, closing the door behind him. As soon as he's gone, my shoulders slump and I relax again. Then I remember I still need a shower and head into the bathroom, which is still steamy from when he used it. The room smells faintly of pine too, which makes me wonder if his skin smells as good, and then I wonder what it'd be like to press my face into that wet, naked chest, and then I think of him looking at me with those hard blue eyes and now I'm so turned on I can barely think straight.

I turn on the shower and make it cold, because these thoughts? They need to stop.

Except once I'm under the water I can't stop thinking about our exchange. How can I be so comfortable around Luke and Matt, while Shane ties me up in knots? Maybe it's because I get the feeling he doesn't like me so I end up trying super hard with him, which only makes me even more awkward. Luke said that wasn't the case at all though, and that Shane liked me *too* much. That makes no sense though. Shane was the one who insisted upon—and wrote!—the roommate contract. If he wanted me, he wouldn't have done that or made us all sign it.

Unless he just didn't want the other guys to have me...

CHAPTER ELEVEN

ALLIE

ON SATURDAY I spend the afternoon shopping with Brooke. Or rather, hanging out with her while she shops. I'm still broke as fuck, of course.

While Brooke tries on another pair of black heels, she asks, "How's it been living with three guys for the past week?"

I admire a pair of flats I can't afford. "Good, actually. The house is amazing. And the guys are all pretty cool, especially for actors. Except for..."

"Except for my brother."

"Yeah." I put down the shoes with a sigh. "He's letting me live rent-free so I can't complain."

"Sure you can. My brother is a grade A dick."

"I'm not sure I'd go that far." And now I'm thinking about his dick. That towel did not hide the shape of his large package and my imagination is really good at running wild. And trust me, it wants to get wild...with him. "He's just hard to get to know."

"I can tell you everything you need to know about him." She slides off the shoes and tries on another pair that are almost identical. I wish she'd add some color, but she and I have very different feelings about that. "Ask me anything."

"That's too weird, like you're giving away his secrets." Except I do want to know all his secrets. Every dirty one of them. Ugh, what is wrong with me?

"Fine. But promise me you're not getting all heart-eyes over him. Or the other guys, for that matter."

"Um...no?" I say, but it doesn't sound convincing even to me.

She stops and gives me a fierce stare. "You are, aren't you? Which one?"

"Uh. I kind of like...all of them." I duck my head.

Her eyes widen. "Oh, shit. You're really in trouble."

"I know. Trust me, I know."

"Just be careful, Allie. I don't want you getting your heart broken again. Getting involved with any one of them is a terrible idea. Having feelings for all of them is a total disaster."

Don't I know it.

When I get home, her warning is still in my head. I park my beat-up old Ford Focus in the giant four-car garage, and as I gaze at the other three shining, expensive cars next to it, it's a good reminder that I don't belong here. Not with Shane and his Tesla Model X. Not with Luke and his Audi R8 Spyder. And not with Matt and his BMW 230 convertible either.

I head back to my room, but when I sit on my bed and slip off my shoes I hear laugher from outside. Through the window I spot Luke walking by the pool and my heart skips, which Brooke would definitely not approve of. He must have returned from his quick trip to London.

I make my way outside, irresistibly drawn toward the low male voices and the sound of splashing water. When I step onto the patio, I'm faced with something from one of my naughtiest fantasies. All three guys are in the pool, wearing nothing but swim trunks. My mouth falls open and my eyes widen, drinking in the sight of all that wet, muscular, tanned skin on display. I don't even know where to look. All three of them are so delicious, there's no way I can choose. It's like a buffet of men and I want to sample each one. Repeatedly.

No! This is not a buffet, this is a window display at Tiffany's. Strictly look-don't-touch, and if you need to ask the price, you can't afford it anyway.

"Hey guys," I say, but my voice comes out a little husky. I clear my throat.

"Allie!" Matt says, bursting up from the water in front of me. "You should join us!"

I want to. I really want to. But getting in the pool with them sounds like a really dangerous idea. I can already picture their wet skin sliding against mine. So much temptation.

Also, if I'm honest with myself, I'm hesitant to get in a swimsuit around these three. I'm not usually shy about my body and I love my curves. I fully believe all bodies are swimsuit bodies. But that doesn't mean I'm comfortable showing mine off to three guys who are used to hanging out with the most beautiful women in the world, all of whom are a lot thinner than me.

"Maybe some other time." I sit on one of the lounge chairs and stretch my feet out. Even if I can't join them in the pool, I can enjoy the sun shining down on me and the breeze against my skin. And best of all, the sight of the three guys in front of me. "I wish I could Instagram this. People would go crazy at the sight of all three of you in a pool together."

Shane's face darkens. "No social media pics."

I roll my eyes. "I know, I know, the roommate contract. I'm just kidding. But seriously, think how many followers I would get!"

"Sorry, this sight is for your eyes only," Luke says, as he flexes his muscles with a grin.

"Lucky me." I swallow and tear my eyes away from his arms. "How was your trip?"

"Busy, but quick." He flicks back his wet hair in one sexy maneuver. "How was your day?"

"Good. I went shopping with Brooke. Or I watched her shop, anyway."

"How is my sister doing?" Shane asks, his tone stiff.

"She's okay. She's been super busy at work and she had a crappy date the other night, but nothing a little retail therapy can't fix."

"You sure you won't come in with us?" Matt asks, with a flirty smile. "We won't bite. Unless you're into that, of course."

I laugh, while Shane glares at him. "Very tempting, but I don't think I could handle all three of you."

"Oh, I bet you could," Luke says, with a voice that promises all sorts of sinful things.

My mind heads straight to porn-land now as I imagine all three guys converging on me in the pool, their hands and mouths moving across my wet, naked skin. Bow chicka wow wow indeed. I'm getting all hot and sweaty thinking about it.

Yep, that's definitely my cue to leave.

"I'll see you guys later," I say, as I stand up. I let my eyes take one last fill of their half-naked bodies to save in my memory for when I'm alone later, then make myself walk away. And then I really hate myself for having such self-restraint.

CHAPTER TWELVE

LUKE

AS I RUN on the treadmill in our gym, my thoughts inevitably wander to Allie. Ever since she moved in, she's been taking over my mind on a regular basis. Seeing her all sad and vulnerable at the bar the other week only made it worse because I related to what she was going through. It was torture being in London, knowing she was back here moping over her ex, and I rushed back to LA as quickly as I could.

It's silly because I barely know her and I can't have her anyway, but I haven't felt like this about anyone in a long time. Not since Lana. The fact that Allie, with her sweet voice and bright smile and tempting curves, can make me forget the only woman I ever loved? That's a goddamn miracle. I want to explore it. To see if my feelings for her are real, or if she's just a delicious little temporary distraction.

Too bad the other guys will kill me if I do anything with her. Oh, Shane tries to act like he isn't interested, but he's not fooling anyone. And while Matt is a flirt who sleeps with a new woman every other night, I sense something different in my brother when he's around Allie. He likes her too, as more than a one night stand. I haven't seen him bring home any women since she moved in either.

The three of us have been good friends for years and roommates for a few months. I worry that bringing Allie in might disrupt everything between us and ruin our friendship. If we all want her, it could tear us apart...because we can't all have her.

Or can we?

I'm distracted from my thoughts when she walks into the gym, wearing a thin yellow dress that hugs her voluptuous body, with her wet hair hanging about her bare shoulders. I haven't seen her since she vanished yesterday while we were in the pool, her cheeks flushed with heat like she was thinking all sorts of naughty thoughts. Probably the same ones I was thinking. I'd put money on it that the other guys shared the same fantasies as well.

"Hey, Luke," she says, her voice cheerful as usual. She's like a ray of sunshine in my otherwise dark life.

I hit pause on the treadmill and slow my steps. "Hey."

I'm not wearing a shirt—clothes are overrated, in my opinion—and she tries really hard not to stare at my chest, but is having a difficult time keeping her eyes away. It's adorable. She has such an open, honest face and those dimples only make it cuter. It's obvious she's attracted to me and the other guys, but wants to fight it. Just like it's obvious when she's thinking about her ex and is in pain. Like now.

"Um. Sorry to bother you but I was wondering if you have a hair dryer? I'd ask the other guys, but they're out and I don't want to riffle through their bathrooms without their permission."

"I'm sure we've got one somewhere." I step off the treadmill and grab a towel to wipe the sweat off my body. Her hungry eyes follow my every movement so I take my time, making sure she gets a nice long look. "What happened to yours?"

"I, uh..." She finally glances away, biting her lip. "I left it at my ex's place."

"We could get you a new one." I sense she isn't telling me something from the way she's avoiding my eyes. "What's wrong, Allie?"

She blows out a long breath. "I left a lot of stuff at my ex's place, not just the blow dryer. I was so upset when he told me I had to leave that I grabbed whatever I could and threw it in my car and ran. But now I'm so annoyed at myself because I need some of those things and I don't have the money to replace it all yet. But I will. It's not a problem. I'll be fine, I swear."

Conflicting emotions war within me. Desire for her. Anger at her ex. And now, protectiveness and a need to take care of her. "I can buy you anything you want. I'm sure the other guys would be happy to help also."

She stares down at the floor. "I don't want your charity. I already owe you all so much."

"You don't owe us anything." I slide my fingers under her chin, drawing her gaze back to me. "But you're right. It's better if you get back your old stuff anyway."

Her eyes widen. "What? No!"

"Why not?"

"I can't go back to the apartment. What if his new girlfriend is there? Oh god." She shakes her head vigorously. "No way. I can't face him again."

"This is exactly what you need to do to get closure. Once you face him, you'll finally be able to move on."

She scrunches up her face. "Do you really think so?"

"I know so. Trust me on this. I've gone through it myself."

"Maybe you're right."

"You don't have to do it alone either. I'll go with you."

Her eyes light up. "Really? You'd do that for me?"

I stroke her cheek with my fingers, thinking I'd do anything she asked of me right now. Any damn thing. "I would."

"Thank you." She wraps her arms around me and pulls me in for a tight hug. The feel of her soft body against my naked chest is enough to make my dick rise to attention, especially as I breathe in her hair, which smells like coconut. I hold her close, not wanting to ever let her go.

I'm about to press my lips to her neck and say fuck it to the roommate contract, when Shane's voice stops me cold.

"What's going on in here?" he asks from the doorway.

Allie pulls out of my arms and turns toward him. "Luke's going to help me get my things back from my ex."

Shane's scowl intensifies and he glares at me like he's mad I got to hold her first. I grin back at him like the cocky bastard I am.

"I'm going with you," Shane says.

"Where are we going?" Matt asks, joining us in the gym.

"We're taking a trip to visit Allie's ex to get her stuff back," I say.

Matt cracks his knuckles with a devious grin. "Perfect. I was hoping for some excitement tonight."

"You really don't all need to come," Allie says, glancing between us. A slight smile touches her lips. "Although I'm not saying no either. Parker won't know what hit him if I show up with all three of you."

"He will if he tries something," I growl. "When my fist hits his face."

Matt rolls his eyes. "Rein it in, big guy."

"I'm with Luke," Shane says. "That asshole deserves to be taught a lesson."

"No one is going to teach anyone a lesson," Allie says. "I just want my blow dryer back."

I give her arm a squeeze. "And we're going to get it for you. Right now."

CHAPTER THIRTEEN

ALLIE

BY THE TIME we pull up outside the apartment I used to share with Parker, it's already gotten dark. I gaze up at the window of my former living room, which is brightly lit, meaning he—or his new girlfriend—must be inside. Or even worse, both of them together. Barf.

"I can't do this," I say, speaking around the giant lump that's formed in my throat.

Shane gives me a stern look from the driver's seat of his Tesla. "Yes, you can."

I can't breathe. I think I might seriously start hyperventilating. "Maybe you can drive around the block a few times."

He scowls at me. "I'm not doing that."

Luke rests his large hand on my shoulder from the seat behind me. "We'll be with you the entire time."

"We've got your back, Allie," Matt adds.

Okay. I can do this. I can face Parker. I can get my stuff back.

I throw open the car door and leap out before I lose my nerve. The three guys follow me, their doors slamming behind me as I stalk toward the apartment complex. When I get to the gate I nearly turn around, except I know my roommates won't let me. Having them at my back gives me the courage to enter the gate code, which I still remember. With a faint buzz, it opens.

We head into the courtyard of the apartment complex, which is a small, square area dotted with grass, olive trees, and pink flowers. I brush past it all and climb the stairs. I'm on a mission now, like a princess with her three knights sent to take down a dragon and steal his treasure.

No. *My* treasure.

When we reach the door to my old apartment, I take a second to draw in a breath and gather my strength. Shane gives me an encouraging nod, Matt offers me a warm smile, and Luke looks like he might tear the door down himself if I don't.

I ring the doorbell.

The next few moments last a lifetime. I nearly turn around and bolt. I swear I age three years in the pause before when the door finally opens, revealing Parker on the other site.

"Allie," he says. "What are you doing here?"

He's wearing jeans and the pale blue shirt I got him for Christmas. My heart clenches with pain, remembering how happy we were that day, but then I fight it off.

"I'm here to get the rest of my stuff."

His brow furrows. "I didn't realize you left anything here."

"Well, I did. Can we come in?"

"Uh, yeah," he says as he opens the door. "Who are these people?"

"We're the guys she's living with now," Matt says.

"You can see she traded up," Luke adds.

I brush past Parker, whose mouth is hanging open at the sight of the three tall actors, and step into my old apartment. Since I gave up my own place to move in with him, most of the furniture isn't mine. Still it brings back memories of all the time we spent in this apartment together. Watching TV on the couch. Making breakfast together on Sundays. Playing card games with friends at the dining table. All things I will never do with him again.

"Wait," Parker says, glancing between the three men. "You're Luke Hart. Like from the *Death Strikes* movies." His eyes somehow get even bigger as he takes this all in. "And Shane Easton from *Talon*. Holy crap. I watch that show every week."

Matt raises his eyebrows, like he's waiting to be recognized, but then sighs dramatically. "Come on, Allie. Let's get your crap so we can get out of here."

Fine with me. I start in the bathroom, grabbing my blow dryer first. Matt follows me inside with a packing box in hand and stands there while I go through every drawer and cabinet, pulling out anything I bought. This time, I won't be rushed.

The bedroom is next, although I can barely stand to enter it. It reminds me of all the good times we had in there, but also that he probably screws his new girlfriend there in our bed. Oddly, there's no trace of her in the apartment. No lipstick tubes, no high heels, no pictures of them together. Nothing.

The other guys follow me in to the bedroom and Shane offers another empty box. I pull out some clothes I left behind, along with a pair of tennis shoes I find in the back of the closet, then point at the TV. "That's mine too."

"Wait—" Parker starts, but Shane cuts him off with a sharp glare.

"I paid for it. Therefore, it's coming with me." Damn, it feels good to stand up to him.

"We'll get it," Luke says.

As I check the closet for anything I missed, Luke and Matt unplug the TV and lift it easily, then carry it out of the apartment while Parker gapes at us like he can't believe this is happening. I search the living room and kitchen—finding my favorite spatula and muffin tin—and then I'm done.

"That's it," I tell Shane. "Could you give us a moment please?"

"Fine," he says with a frown. "But I'll be right outside if you need me."

As soon as he steps out, Parker asks, "What's going on, Allie? You live with those guys now?"

"Yeah, I do." I glance around the apartment again. "Where's your new girlfriend?"

He rubs the back of his neck and won't meet my eyes. "She uh...decided not to move in with me after all."

"Figures." I start for the door, but then stop. Luke's words about closure echo in my brain. This is my last chance to get it. I turn around. "Why did you do it?"

"Because I'm an idiot," he says, his face falling. "I gave up the best thing in my life for a stupid fling. I'm sorry."

"You *are* an idiot. But I'm glad you cheated on me so I found out what a dickhead you are now and not after we were married. I just wish I hadn't wasted a year of my life on you." I open the door. "Goodbye, Parker."

I step outside, where my three roommates are waiting for

me, and my shoulders relax. I was so worried about facing Parker again, but now I feel vindicated—and like I can breathe for the first time in days. Luke was right, this was a good idea.

I smile at the three men holding my stuff. "Let's go home."

CHAPTER FOURTEEN

ALLIE

WE RETURN HOME TRIUMPHANT, like the underdog sports team in a sappy movie right after they finally won the big game against their rivals. After the guys help me bring all my stuff in, Shane pops open a bottle of red wine, while the rest of us spread out around the living room. I get comfortable on one of the boxy white couches, while Shane sits beside me and begins pouring wine for all of us. The two Hart brothers lounge around me on the other furniture, effortlessly moving into Instagram-worthy poses that somehow look both sexy and casual. Genetics, man. So unfair.

"How are you feeling, Allie?" Luke asks.

"Like a huge weight has been lifted off my shoulders." I smile at him and then the other guys. "Thanks for all your help tonight."

"It was nothing," Shane says.

"That guy was a tool," Matt says, raising his glass. "Good riddance."

"Yes, he was. I think I can finally move on now." I take a

slow sip of my wine and let it warm me up. "But enough about Parker. I'm done letting him take up space in my brain. Let's talk about something else."

"Like what?" Matt asks.

I swirl my glass as I consider. "Hmm. How did you all meet?"

"This guy?" Matt says, pointing his wine at Luke. "I have no idea who this guy is."

Luke grabs his little brother in a rough hug and messes up his hair, while Matt groans. I love seeing them together. It reminds me of being with my older sister.

Shane shakes his head at them. "I met Matt in an improv class."

"Improv?" I let out a surprised laugh.

Matt yanks away from his brother with a grin. "Yep. The one thing Shane is terrible at."

Shane scowls and pours himself more wine. "I took it as a way to keep from losing my mind while I was in law school. Or perhaps to piss off my parents. As Matt says, it wasn't my favorite thing, but we became roommates after that. I met Luke through him a year later."

"I know Shane and Brooke grew up in Los Angeles, but what about you two?" I ask the brothers.

"Our family's in Kansas," Luke says. "I moved here the minute I finished college. Matt followed me two years later."

"Wow, that must have been a big change for you."

"Definitely. It was rough at first. I was just another dumb kid moving to LA to try to become an actor, working as a waiter on the side. Sometimes I'm amazed it worked out."

"For one of us anyway," Matt mutters.

Luke clasps him on the shoulder. "Your time will come."

"What do your parents think of that?" I asked.

"They're proud of us." Luke shrugs. "But they'd be proud no matter what we did."

"Mine are like that too," I say. "But—"

Then I shriek when I see a spider crawl across the couch beside me. I jump up and back into the glass windows, nearly spilling my wine in the process. "Get it away from me!"

All three guys stare at me like I'm completely nuts. "Are you all right?" Shane asks.

"Spider!" I point at it, then cover my eyes. "Oh god, I can't look."

Luke bursts out into loud, friendly laughter, and Matt joins in too. When I peek, even Shane is smirking.

I stomp my foot. "This is serious!"

That only makes them laugh even harder. "Your face," Matt says, doubling over.

"It's just a small spider," Shane says, shaking his head. "But I'll take care of it."

"Thank you." I refuse to inch any closer until he retrieves a paper towel and gets rid of the vicious monster.

Luke chuckles. "So when you said you were deathly afraid of spiders, you weren't kidding."

"I always have been." I shudder. "They're just so creepy."

"Don't worry, we'll keep you safe," Matt says, with a flirty smile.

"All you did was laugh at me!" Now that the threat is gone, my heart rate is slowing down to normal levels again and I can laugh it off. "Shane's the only one who was willing to save me." I sit back down beside him and flutter my eyelashes at him dramatically. "My brave defender."

Heat sparks between us as our eyes meet, but then he

clears his throat and looks away with a frown. "It was just a spider. Don't make a big deal out of it." He abruptly rises to his feet. "I've got an early morning. Good night."

My heart sinks as he storms off. Every time I think the two of us are forming a connection, he shoots me down.

"Don't mind him," Luke says. "Shane is always prickly."

I force a smile. "It's fine. But I'm going to head to bed too. Thanks again for all your help tonight."

"It was our pleasure," Matt says. "And if you need company in bed..."

I roll my eyes with a laugh. "You wish."

I leave the guys behind and head downstairs. Shane's door is closed, but the light is on. I consider knocking and saying something to him, but decide it's best to let him be. Instead, I head into my room and survey all the boxes with my reclaimed stuff in them, along with my TV on the dresser. With a big, relieved sigh I throw myself on the bed and sink into the lush sheets. My relationship with Parker is truly over and for once I'm not sad about it anymore. That chapter of my life is over—and a new one is starting now, right here in this house. I can't wait to turn the page and see what happens next.

CHAPTER FIFTEEN

ALLIE

BROOKE NUDGES me with her beer. "Check it out. Hot guy at six o'clock."

I swivel around to look at the guy she's eyeing, who's standing at the bar and ordering a drink from Matt. "You're right, he is hot. I'm so proud of you for noticing."

"I know what you like, even if I'd rather be looking at that woman in the corner with the tattooed arms." She nudges me again. "Go on. Go talk to him."

"No way." It's been a week since I got my stuff back from Parker, and I decided I was ready to venture out to meet men again, this time with Brooke in tow. Only problem is, the one guy in here I want is Matt and he's not on the menu. For me, anyway. Other women are flirting with him left and right, making my blood boil.

Ugh, maybe coming to this bar again was a mistake.

"Why not?" Brooke asks. "You said you were ready to get back out there."

As Matt flashes a blond woman a flirty smile while pouring

her a drink, jealousy simmers inside me. "Fine, I'll go talk to him *if* you go talk to that girl you've been checking out for the last ten minutes."

Brooke shakes her head. "I don't have time for a relationship right now."

"You have time to hang out in a bar with me."

"That's different. You're my favorite person in the world, other than myself, of course. I'll always make time for you." Her eyes flick back to the tattooed woman, who takes a sip of her drink and flashes a come-hither smile at Brooke. "Besides, we're trying to get you some rebound sex. That guy is perfect."

I glance over at the guy again. He's definitely handsome, with neatly trimmed dark hair, a clean-shaven face, and a good smile. He looks like a nice guy, but not *too* nice, if you know what I mean. But he's only a few inches taller than me and he's a bit scrawny for my tastes. I'm not exactly a small girl, after all. In fact, I'm pretty sure I could crush him. At least Parker had enough meat on his bones that I didn't think I'd hurt him if I was on top. And the guys I'm living with now, well, any one of which could probably pick me up and bang me in the middle of this room without breaking a sweat.

Just as I shove that delicious image to the back of my mind, Shane himself walks in, his eyes scouring the room until they rest on me. My hackles instantly rise and I down the rest of my drink, then glance back at the new guy at the bar.

"What do I do?" I ask Brooke.

"Go over there and talk to him."

"Just like that?"

"Yep. Just like that."

"Okay. I'm going in." I stand up, fix my skirt, adjust my

boobs, and walk over to him like I'm going into battle. I have no idea what I'll say, but when does that ever stop me?

I'm pretty sure Shane and Matt both watch the entire time, but that only spurs me on. As I approach the guy at the bar, I flash him my most dazzling smile and he grins back at me. I'm pretty sure I weigh double what he weighs, but it's fine. I won't judge him by his size, like I hope he won't judge me by mine. We'll just make sure he's on top.

"Hi there," the guy says, as I slide onto the barstool next to him. "I haven't seen you in here before."

"This is only my second time coming here."

"Must be my lucky night." He offers his hand. "I'm Keith."

I shake his hand. "Allie."

"Let me get you a drink." He waves Matt over with a casual smile.

Matt stops in front of us and gives a forced grin I've never seen before, like he's gritting his teeth the entire time. "What'll it be?"

"Another strawberry lemoncello martini," I tell him.

"Coming right up." He glares at the guy flirting with me, then turns away to make my drink.

Shane is also shooting daggers at the guy from where he sits with Brooke. I'm honestly surprised they care so much. They could have almost any woman in here—hell, they could have most women in Los Angeles and quite a few men too—but they're acting like they want *me*. Even after making me sign a contract saying they couldn't have me.

Talk about an ego boost. For the first time since Parker I feel sexy, confident, and desired. Even if I have no real interest in Keith, I've got to keep this going.

"So what do you do, Allie?" Keith asks.

"I'm a high school English teacher. What about you?"

"I'm an accountant."

We chit chat for the next fifteen minutes, but I barely listen to a word he says. Matt brings me a drink and when his fingertips brush against my knuckles as he hands it to me, I swear he does it on purpose. Brooke finally goes to chat with the tattooed woman in the corner, leaving Shane sitting alone, looking all broody and hot in his booth as he tries very hard to not watch me with this guy.

By the time Keith leaves, I've got his number and a date with him tomorrow night. I flash a triumphant smile at Matt. "You were right. I did need to get out and have a little fun."

"Good for you," he says, but he doesn't sound like he means it. He turns his back to me as he makes another drink.

I grab my martini and head over to the booth before Shane's laser beam eyes burn through my back. I'm hoping Brooke will save me from the awkwardness, but when I glance over, she's making out with that girl. Guess I'm on my own then.

"What was that about?" Shane asks, his voice dripping with disdain.

"I'm just doing what Matt suggested and getting back out there again."

His eyes narrow. "You should know by now to never listen to Matt."

A sexy giggle from the corner draws our attention to Brooke and her new fling. "Looks like your sister is getting lucky tonight," I say with a grin.

"Good. She works too much."

"So do you." I barely ever see Shane during the week. He's up at the crack of dawn and doesn't return home 'til late. For some reason it makes me sad, even though when we're together we seem to mostly butt heads.

"Our shooting schedule is brutal at the moment because we're doing a crossover with another show. It should calm down next week. The crew loved the muffins by the way. Thanks for that."

"You're welcome," I say, feeling all warm from his praise. "Did you always know you wanted to be an actor?" For once, Shane is talking to me like a civilized person. I'm not letting this chance to learn more about him slip by.

"No." He stirs his drink slowly. "I originally planned to be a lawyer."

"Like Brooke."

"Like our entire family." His jaw clenches. "I always loved acting but my parents never approved of it, and I never considered pursing it as a career. I finished law school, passed the BAR exam, and then Matt convinced me to audition with him for a small role in a TV show, mostly to keep him company that day. Then I got the part. No one was more surprised than I was. And my parents never forgave me."

"Wow. Do you ever regret giving up a legal career?"

"Never. I hated law school. I only did it because my parents made it clear that's what the Eastons did. Acting was always my secret passion and now I get to do it and get paid for it. Win-win."

"And your parents?" I ask.

He smirks. "Oh, they barely talk to me."

"I'm sorry. But hey, at least they have one child who is a lawyer."

"Yes. Although she ruined it by being gay." He chuckles, a

low sound that is sexier than anything. "My sister and I are both disappointments to our parents."

"You're both following your hearts. Your parents will have to come to terms with that."

"If only it were so easy." He tilts his head as he considers me. "I suppose your parents were the kind who always encouraged you to do whatever you want."

"Yep. Mom is a professor, dad is a vet. We grew up with books and animals. Guess it's no surprise I became an English teacher and my sister became a vet."

"You're lucky." It seems like he might say more, but then he downs the rest of his drink and stands up. "I'll see you back at the house."

I watch him go with a touch of sadness. Once again, just when I think the two of us might be bonding, he takes off. It's clear he doesn't like me and is counting down the days 'til I find my own place.

Why do I even bother with him?

CHAPTER SIXTEEN

SHANE

NADIA STEPS FORWARD and rests her hand on my bare chest. "I know who you really are. *What* you really are. But I don't care. I still want to be with you."

Her lips touch mine and all I feel is revulsion. It's hard to believe a few months ago I enjoyed kissing her, when all I want to do now is rinse my mouth out the second this is over. There's no tongue action, but we make it look passionate for the camera, even though we can barely stand to be near each other. When the director yells, "Cut!" it's a damn mercy.

Nadia and I practically leap apart, and she sneers at me as I slide my arm across my mouth to wipe the taste away. Cherries, that's what she tastes like. I can't stand them anymore. Another thing she's ruined for me forever.

Not to mention, there's only one woman I want to be kissing, and it sure as hell isn't her.

"We both know you miss these lips," Nadia says, as she pours antibacterial gel all over her hands. "I can tell every time we kiss."

I give her a scathing look. "It's called acting. You should try it sometime."

Jackson, our director, sighs at me and Nadia like we're kids who are misbehaving. "You two, take a break. And when you come back, I want your A game."

I give him a sharp nod and head toward the door leading outside, where my trailer waits. But I'm stopped by one of our executive producers, Martin.

"Shane. A word, please?"

Inside Martin's office, two other producers are inside, Wendy and Liam. I have a sudden flashback to being called in to the principal's office as a kid.

"Have a seat, Shane," Martin says. He doesn't sit though, just props himself up on the cabinet behind his desk. A power position, my father would say. I decide to remain standing.

"I'm fine. What's this about?"

Martin's lips press together when he sees I won't sit. "We wanted to talk with you about Nadia."

"Specifically about you and Nadia," Wendy adds.

"There is no me and Nadia. Not anymore."

"That's the problem," Liam says.

I cross my arms. "It's not an issue."

"We disagree, and so does the network," Martin says. "The two of you used to have great chemistry. Then everything changed at the end of last season."

I give him a stare that I hope conveys how much a waste of time I find this conversation to be. "You know what she did."

He waves his hand. "Yes, of course. But at the end of last season, ratings were down and viewers weren't happy."

"I'm not sure how that's my fault," I grit out.

Wendy folds her hands in her lap and speaks patiently.

"We spent two seasons building the romance between your characters, but then after you got together the relationship felt flat because it was obvious to everyone that you two hated each other."

"What exactly are you saying?" I ask.

"Nadia's talking about leaving the show," Martin says. "Maybe doing a spinoff series for the network."

"Good riddance. We don't need her anyway."

"The network disagrees," Liam says. "They're threatening to cut our show order. Twelve episodes instead of twenty-four."

Every muscle in my body tenses. "They can't do that."

"And if that happens, you can guarantee this will be our last season," Martin says.

"We're fighting for the show," Wendy says, her voice calm. "But you need to prove to everyone that you and Nadia can work together. Viewers want romance, even on a superhero show. You have to give that to them. Either it needs to spark again, or we need to figure something else out to save our show."

I run a frustrated hand through my hair. "What am I supposed to do? You've seen how she is."

Martin gives me an even look. "Figure it out. Talk to her. Go to therapy. Get back together with her if you have to. I don't fucking care. But if you don't, we're all going to be out of a job in a few months."

They dismiss me and I storm out of the office, past the makeup department where Nadia is getting touched up, and out the door to the lot. As the star of the show, my trailer is the biggest one, and I throw open the door with a loud bang.

"I'm guessing the kissing scene went as well as expected

then," Hannah says, from her spot on the leather couch inside. She's Asian, gorgeous, and the only person who makes work tolerable these days. Her legs are propped up on my table, but I'm used to it by now.

"Even worse," I say, as I head to the mini bar. "The producers all called me in for a meeting."

Hannah sits up straight, her long black hair falling around her shoulders. She's not in her geeky hot outfit anymore, which means she must be done shooting for the day. Hannah plays Jenna, a hacker and the best friend of my character—Talon—on the show. "What did they want?"

I pour myself a vodka and slump onto the couch across from her. "This season is going to be our last unless I can work shit out with Nadia."

"Holy crap. What are you going to do?"

I run through my options as I sip my drink. Getting back together with Nadia is not an option, especially when I can't stop thinking about Allie all day long. There's got to be some other way to save the show, but I'm coming up blank so far.

"Damned if I know," I finally say. "But I'll figure something out."

I have to.

CHAPTER SEVENTEEN

ALLIE

THIS HOUSE IS FREEZING. I don't understand why I need to wear a sweater in my bedroom when it's 85 degrees outside. I blame Shane. He gave me strict orders not to touch the thermostat, which he keeps set to Arctic levels even when he isn't here all day.

No more.

I creep upstairs like a burglar until I find the controls, then adjust the temp from 65—seriously, his electric bill must be ridiculous!—to 75. I'll have to make sure to change it back before he gets home.

When I'm back in my room I turn on my TV (the one we rescued from Parker) as background noise while I get ready for my date with Keith tonight. An episode of Shane's show *Talon* is airing, one from the beginning of last season. I check the guide and discover they're running an entire marathon of it in preparation for the new season starting soon.

Is it weird that I'm watching my roommate's TV show when he isn't here? It almost feels voyeuristic, like I'm spying on him at work. I've seen a few episodes before—Parker watches it—but now it's different because I actually know Shane.

I can't turn it off though. I tell myself it's a good way to get to know him better. Not to mention, he's shirtless a lot in *Talon*. There's no way I can pass that up.

I quickly get sucked into the show and before I know it I'm sitting cross-legged on the bed with my mouth open as Shane's character Talon makes up with Nadia's character Diana after she found out he's a superhero and realized he's been lying to her for a year about it. Shane pulls Nadia against him and crushes his lips to hers in a passionate kiss. I'm both jealous and turned on, because from what I can see he is a damn fine kisser.

My door flies open and I shriek. Shane looms in my doorway and I hit a button on the TV to hide what I'm watching, but that only makes it worse because the screen pauses on a close-up of him and Nadia kissing.

"You touched the thermostat," he says, his voice like steel.

"Um. Yes. But in my defense it was really cold in here and no one else was home."

"Don't touch it again." His gaze travels to the TV and his eyes harden at the sight of him and Nadia. His mouth twists, as if he's disgusted that I'm watching his show. "And turn that off."

He storms out of the room without another word. I should probably let him go, but I'm tired of him treating me like this. Since facing Parker, I'm more confident than ever. Besides, Shane and I connected last night. Or at least I thought we did.

I get up and chase after him, into the hallway between our rooms. "What, am I not allowed to watch your show either?"

He turns back to me with a scowl on his gorgeous lips. His piercing blue eyes drift down to my red vintage dress that hugs my body and ends right above the knee. "Are you going out?"

"I have a date," I say, standing up a little taller.

His eyes narrow. "With that guy from last night?"

"That's the one."

"You can't go." His tone leaves no room for argument.

I blink at him. "Why not?"

He doesn't answer, only stares at me with so much heated intensity I worry the carpet under us might spontaneously combust. He looks at me like he wants to tear me apart...and also tear off all my clothes.

I huff. "I'm sorry I messed with your precious thermostat. And I'm sorry I was watching your show, even though it's really good. And I'm sorry you have a stick up your ass all the damn time." I put my hands on my hips and face him down. "But you know what I'm not sorry for? Having a damn date. Now if you'll excuse me, I need to finish getting ready."

I turn away, but he catches my hand and pulls me back to him. Before I know what's happening, his arm slides behind my waist, his other hand tangles in my hair, and his mouth is on mine.

He kisses me hard, with an angry, fiery passion, like he's trying to win our fight with his lips and his tongue. I give it back to him just as good, my fingers tight on his jaw, my body pressed close against his. We kiss like we want to devour each other.

"This is why you can't go," he says, before capturing my mouth again. I'm immediately swept away, desire unfurling throughout my entire body as he gives me a kiss that puts his one with Nadia to shame.

I somehow come to my senses and push him away. "What about the roommate contract?"

"Fuck the roommate contract." He presses me back against the wall, one hand over my head while he leans in and kisses me again, like he can't bear to stop now that he's started. I let him tilt my head, possessing me with his hands and his lips and his entire body. I'm trapped, but there's nowhere else I want to be.

He finally releases my lips and I sigh, but then his mouth is trailing down my jaw to my neck. He inhales me like a drug, practically nipping at my skin as he kisses his way down to my collarbone. All I can do is relent to his control, while he takes his time tasting me. Damn, if Shane is this good a kisser, I can only imagine what it'd be like to be in bed with him.

"What the fuck?" Matt's voice says behind us.

Oh shit.

CHAPTER EIGHTEEN

ALLIE

MY EYES POP open and I glance over at Matt, horrified. Luke stands beside him. Both of them are shooting daggers at Shane with their eyes, and a hot rush floods my cheeks.

Shane lifts his head lazily from my neck and glares at the guys. "Do you mind?"

"Yeah, we fucking mind," Luke says.

"You made us sign your stupid roommate contract and now you're the one breaking it?" Matt asks. "Seriously?"

I push Shane away and he reluctantly takes a step back, allowing me to catch my breath. All three guys are glaring now, their bodies tense as if they might tackle each other to the floor right in front of me. I have to fix this somehow or I'm going to be out of a home again. More than that, I don't want these men I care about to be fighting with each other.

"I'm so sorry," I tell them, even though I don't really have anything to apologize for. For one thing, Shane kissed me. For another, I can kiss whoever the hell I want. Yet I still feel guilty, like I somehow cheated on Matt and Luke, which is silly because I'm not *with* any of them.

"Looks like Shane only had us sign that contract to make sure he got to her first," Luke says to his brother, his voice a low growl.

Shane crosses his arms. "It wasn't like that at all."

I nod quickly. "We were fighting and it just kind of happened. It was only one kiss. Really."

"That looked like more than kissing to me," Luke mumbles.

Matt's gaze turns to me, with heat in his eyes. "If I'd known kissing you was on the table, I would have done it ages ago."

My eyebrows dart up. "Really?"

Shane rolls his eyes at all of us. "I'll tear up the roommate contract right now. Will that make you two feel better?"

"Not really," Luke says. "You broke the rules and have an unfair advantage in winning her over now."

"Winning me over?" I ask, not quite believing my ears.

"What about the clause in there about what happens if someone breaks the contract?" Matt asks.

Shane stiffens. "I shouldn't have put that in there."

"What clause?" I ask.

Matt arches an eyebrow. "The clause that says if one roommate does something with you, the other two can do the same thing in the sake of fairness."

"Only if both parties are interested," Shane adds.

"*What?*" I practically yell. "I don't remember agreeing to that!"

"It was at the bottom of the contract," Shane says, with a lazy shrug.

I can't decide if I'm offended, horrified, or really excited and turned on by this new twist. "So what you're saying is...to make this right I have to kiss both Matt and Luke. If they want to, that is."

"Oh, they definitely want to," Shane says, glaring at them again.

Luke's glower is just as intense. "Hey, you're the one who wrote the contract, and you're the one who broke it. Don't blame us for this mess."

"Fine. If Allie kisses both of you, we'll be even," Shane says. "Then we can drop this entire thing. Happy?"

"All right," Luke says, while Matt nods.

"And you're okay with this?" I ask Shane incredulously.

Shane drags a hand through his lush, dark blond hair with a scowl. "I'd rather keep you to myself, but I also want everyone in this house to get along, and it does seem like this is the best way to keep the peace here."

Keep the peace, maybe. Or more likely make everything more sexually charged between all of us. But kissing all three guys... I won't lie, the idea sends a rush of desire between my legs. I want all of them, but this seems like a bad idea for so many reasons. I've read enough books to know that love triangles always end badly for someone. And this is a love quadrangle, so it's even worse.

"What happens if it turns into more than kissing?" Matt asks.

"Then everyone else can go that far with her, too," Shane says. "If Allie wants to, of course. We won't make her do anything."

Oh, Allie definitely wants to. The thought of being with all three of them should feel wrong, but instead it feels so very right. Then again, what girl would turn down three of the sexiest men in Hollywood, who all want her for some strange reason?

"Are we agreed then?" Shane asks. He holds out his hand to the others.

"Agreed," Matt and Luke say, as they all shake hands.

I gape at the three of them. "Um, don't I get a say in this?"

Shane turns back to me. "Of course. Nothing will happen without your consent. Are you all right with this plan?"

"Yes. I think so." I bite my lip. "Except... Do I need to kiss Matt and Luke now? In front of you?"

"No," Shane says.

"Good." I take a deep breath, my head spinning. "I'm okay with this, but I need some time to think about all of it. This whole situation is very unusual."

"Take as much time as you need," Luke says.

"I'm guessing you won't be going on that date tonight after all." Shane's lips curl up in a smile that reminds me of a cat after it's caught a mouse. Guess he got what he wanted after all.

"No date," I say. "I have more than I can handle with you three already."

I slip back into my room and close the door, then grab my phone to text Keith that I can't make it after all. There's no sense going out with that guy when I have a real chance with the three guys I actually want. Even though I worry this is only going to end in disaster.

Sure, I can kiss each of them, and maybe do more too. God knows I want that. But then what? I'll eventually have to pick one and that will make things awkward with the others. They've been best friends for a long time, and I don't want to ruin that or cause problems between them.

On the other hand, I won't be living here much longer. Only a few more weeks. I'm attracted to all the guys and for some crazy reason they seem to like me too, which I never would have expected in a million years. Three hot actors lusting after me—any girl would be nuts to pass that opportunity down. Maybe I'll try each of them out, get to know them all a little better, and then I'll be able to decide which one I want to pursue a real relationship with by the time I have to move out. Hopefully the other two guys won't be too upset afterward.

There are only two ways this can end. Me, alone and heartbroken and homeless again, like after Parker dumped me. Or me with one of the guys and not the other two.

I just really wish I didn't have to choose. I want to be with all three of them.

But the guys would never go for that. Would they?

CHAPTER NINETEEN

MATT

I TOSS a script onto the sand next to the rest of them. I have one big pile of hell no's and another pile of scripts I still have to read through. All sent over by my agent, who is also my brother's agent. Yep, I can't even get an agent on my own. I am a pity client.

What does it matter if I even go through all these scripts? None of them want me. They all want my big, famous, older brother. I'm just a sad stand-in for him.

At least the beach is nice and empty today. The weather is perfect, with a warm sun, a cool breeze, and the crisp scent of the ocean in the air. I don't think it can get any better, until Allie walks out onto the beach wearing a short little dress with tiny white dogs printed on it that somehow makes her look both sexy and adorable. I don't know how she manages to rock both at once, but she does. I'm torn between wanting to push her skirt up and running my hands along those thighs, or eating ice cream with her and chatting about anything or nothing at all. I've never wanted both with one girl before—a lover *and* a friend.

"Hey," she says, with an easy smile. "What are you up to?"

"Going through scripts in the hope of finding my next project."

She sinks onto the towel beside me, tucking her feet at her side. "Any luck?"

"Not so far, and it's going to take me a million years to get through all these. Especially since I need to get to the bar soon."

"Need help?" She grabs one of the scripts and riffles through it. "Ooh, this one is set on a cruise ship. That sounds fun."

I raise an eyebrow at her. "You actually think reading these would be fun?"

"Sure. I love reading and I'm off work right now with lots of free time. I'd be happy to help you weed out the good scripts from the bad ones."

"Wow. That would be amazing. I would owe you big time."

"No, you won't. You helped me get my stuff back. This is the least I can do to repay the favor."

"All right, but if you get through one of them and get bored, I won't blame you for quitting."

She playfully shoves me with her shoulder. "I am not a quitter. But is there anything I should look for? Things you're particularly interested in or really don't want?"

I consider for a moment, then shake my head. "I've had such bad luck picking projects for myself, I'd rather have you read them blind and see if you think anything would be good for me."

She nods, her face determined. "Okay, I can do that."

"You're a lifesaver." I wrap an arm around her and bring her in close for a casual hug. Except as I draw her in she turns toward me and rests a hand on my chest, then looks up at me with her beautiful green eyes. I'm usually so smooth with women, but the feel of her in my arms and the way she gazes at me renders me completely helpless.

"Matt," she whispers, her fingers curling into my shirt. "Kiss me."

I don't need to be told twice. I bend my head and coax a slow, teasing kiss from her lips. When I caught her kissing Shane they'd been hot and heavy, making out like they wanted to eat each other alive or possibly kill each other with their mouths—or both. But I'm not Shane, and I want to take my time with Allie. I want to blow her fucking mind. And every other part of her.

Her mouth easily opens for me in invitation, but I don't plunge inside, oh no. I slide my tongue along her lower lip, tasting her slowly, making her gasp into my mouth. Her lips are so soft against mine and I take my time loving them before finally entering her warm mouth with my tongue. I make love to her mouth the same way I plan to make love to her body—thoroughly and deeply, until she's begging me for more.

"Matt," she says in the sexiest voice I've ever heard.

I don't let her speak another word before I take her mouth again. She tightens her grip on my shirt and my hands circle her waist, pulling her closer, until she's in my lap. Straddling me on the beach, our hips flush together, with only our clothes in the way.

My hands begin to roam, finding their way to her thighs. Her dress has ridden up, and it's so easy to run my fingers along her bare skin, higher and higher. She kisses me back like she can't get enough, while stroking my neck and jaw.

When my hands find her ass, I grip it and pull her closer against me. She must feel how hard I am for her, judging from the sweet moan that escapes her lips. My fingers tighten on soft, naked flesh, and I realize she's only wearing a thong.

Oh, fuck me.

But then she breaks the kiss and sits back, gazing at me with lust-filled eyes. "I can't believe we're doing this."

"I can. I've wanted to kiss you from the moment you walked in our front door."

Her cheeks flush and she looks away. "But the other guys..."

"They're not here. We're alone." I use my grip on her ass to rub her against my erection slowly, making us both even more aroused.

"Ohh," she says, closing her eyes as I grind against her. Maybe I'll make her come just like this. Right now I want nothing more than to see her face when she climaxes.

She shakes her head. "This isn't right. It was only supposed to be a kiss. To make things even."

I stop and stare at her, my heart sinking. "Is that the only reason you're kissing me? To even things out between us three?"

"No!" She presses a soft kiss to my lips. "Even before Shane kissed me I wanted to kiss you too. But this is turning into more than kissing..."

I nod, understanding what she means. "And whatever we do, you can do with the other guys."

"Exactly." She tilts her head as she studies my face. "Are you okay with that?"

"I don't know. I've never shared a woman with my best friend and my brother before." I kiss her again, teasing her lower lip with my teeth. "But I think it would be worth it to have you."

She sighs. "I worry this can only end badly."

I want to protest more, to tell her everything will work out somehow, but I'm not sure I believe that.

Before I can stop her, she climbs off my lap and stands up, leaving us both unsatisfied. "I'm sorry," she says. "I don't want to hurt you or the other guys."

"I understand."

And I really do. I can't deny I'm disappointed, because there is nothing I want more than to make her come, preferably with me inside her, but I also don't want to ruin my friendship with the other guys either. Kissing is one thing, sex is another. And while I may have casual sex with women all the time, I get the feeling sex with Allie will be anything but casual.

Sex with her will mean something. I'm not sure I'm ready for that either.

I check the time and sigh. "I need to get to work anyway."

She nods. "I'll start going through these scripts."

I get to my feet and capture her mouth again one more time, unable to resist giving her another kiss. "You're the best."

Then somehow I force myself to walk away from the one woman who's ever made me feel something real.

CHAPTER TWENTY

ALLIE

I'M READING through my third script for Matt when Shane gets home. I can hear him two floors above me in the kitchen, banging around with so much irritation it leaves no doubt it's him and not one of the other guys.

I mark my page in the script and head upstairs before he does anything rash. I've filled the kitchen with all of my cooking supplies and god only knows what he's doing with them. Definitely not cooking, from what I've seen so far.

When I get up there, half of the baking trays are on the counter along with my rice cooker, and he's pulling more things out of another cabinet with vigor.

"What are you doing?" I ask, horrified.

He throws a mixing bowl on the counter, then turns to me. "Where the hell is the blender?"

"Oh, it's over here." I brush past him to the other side of the kitchen and pull out the blender.

"That's not where it goes." He gestures wildly at the kitchen. "How can you find anything in this chaos?"

I glance around, bewildered. "You're the one making a big mess, not me."

"Because nothing is in the right spot! I had everything perfectly organized in here and then you came along and messed it all up!"

It seems our kiss last night was only a temporary ceasefire between us. "I added my own stuff to the mix, that's all." I casually shrug. "I use things and then I put them away where it seems like they should go. It's not my fault if I can't remember your complicated system."

He lets out a frustrated sound and begins grabbing things from the fridge. "It's not complicated. All you have to do is pay a tiny bit of attention and it'd make sense."

"Maybe you can make me a color-coded spreadsheet next time." I cross my arms and watch as he throws fruit and almond milk into the blender. "Don't worry, I'll be out of your hair soon. School starts in a few weeks anyway."

The loud, whirring sound of the blender cuts off any further conversation between us. I silently fume, preparing my next comeback, but when it's done, he turns to me and his face is calmer.

"I'm sorry, Allie. Work has been difficult this week." He hands me the smoothie he made, which is pale pink.

"What's this?" I ask, surprised.

"Strawberry banana." He turns back to the blender to make another one. "Thought you might like it."

"Oh. Thanks." I take a sip. It's really good and totally unexpected. "What's going on at work?"

He blends his smoothie, then turns back to me. "Nadia is making my life hell and the producers are not happy. They're pissed because my chemistry with her is gone." He scowls.

"What did they expect? I walked in on her fucking my stunt double in her trailer."

I nearly choke on my smoothie. "I had no idea."

"No one did. We kept it quiet and out of the press. Just like no one knows that I was so angry I crashed my car into a tree. Brooke covered that up for me."

"Ahh. That's why you owed her a favor."

"Exactly." He practically throws the unused fruit back in the fridge and then slams the door. "And then Nadia had the nerve to say it was my fault she cheated on me. That she didn't think we were serious because she didn't know I actually cared about her."

"Wow." I hesitate. "That's a really shitty thing she did and I am not excusing her at all. But you are kind of hard to read sometimes."

His eyes meet mine and he frowns. "I'm starting to get that, yeah."

"I mean…the other night. And then now." I fumble for words. "It's hard to know where we stand."

He sighs and leans back against the counter, raking a hand through his hair. "I'm sorry about the other night. I'd just heard from the producers that the network is threatening to cancel the show. Then I walked in your room and you were watching that scene with me and her and I couldn't take it."

My eyes widen. "They're threatening to cancel the show? But it's such a good show and I swear I'm not just saying that because we're roommates."

"Thanks. Nadia is talking about leaving the show. I'd be fine with it, but the viewers want romance."

I perk up, hit with a sudden idea. "What about with the hacker girl? Jenna?"

He blinks. "What do you mean?"

"When I was watching the show the other night I was actually rooting for Talon and her to get together. Maybe because she's the geeky, awkward one with glasses and I relate to her a lot more than sleek, sophisticated Diana." I shrug. "I bet there are other fans who feel the same."

He rubs his stubbled jaw as he considers. "That might work. I can talk to the producers about it and see what they think."

I jokingly poke him in the chest. "Just don't get involved with the actress who plays Jenna, or you might have the same problem again."

A sudden laugh rumbles out of him and the sound is so delicious it makes my toes curl. "No need to worry about that. Hannah and I are just friends."

I tilt my head and give him a playful smile. "So I don't need to be jealous then?"

"Of Hannah?" He shakes his head. "Nope. She's only into women."

"Oh. Good."

He moves closer, making me draw in a breath. "And even if she wasn't, you'd have nothing to worry about."

My face flushes and I look away. "There's no reason for me to be jealous anyway. It's not like you belong to me or anything."

His fingers lightly brush against my cheek. "But I could."

My heart skips a beat. "Do you want that?"

"I stopped you from going on that date for a reason. The same reason I kissed you." His hands land on either side of the counter behind me, caging me in with his hard body. "I want you to be mine."

His mouth finds mine, coaxing my lips to open for him before he slowly slides his tongue inside. The angry passion from the other night is gone and he takes his time as he kisses me. My arms slide up around his neck, pulling him closer, wanting even more of him. He groans and lifts me up onto the counter, moving between my legs. It puts me at the exact right height to kiss him without either of us straining and places his hips flush against mine. I can feel his hard length through his slacks and my hands slide down his back to his ass, pulling him closer against me.

"I want to do more than kiss you," he says, as his fingers slip under the hem of my shirt.

I moan into his mouth as his hands roam across my skin. He finds my large breasts, which are heavy with lust for him, and runs his fingers over my already hard nipples through my bra. Red hot desire floods me, making my panties wet for him. I want to do more with him too, so much more, but that means opening the door to so many potential problems. Brooke's warning about falling for the guys runs through my head. I fell for Parker too quickly, and look how that turned out. I don't want to rush into anything now, especially when the situation is even more complicated.

I run my hands along his jaw as I kiss him one last time. "I want more too. But we can't."

His fingers continue rubbing against my nipples in lazy strokes. "You're worried about the other guys."

"Yes."

He sighs and slowly removes his hands from my shirt. "I should never have made the roommate contract."

"Why did you?"

"To protect you. You're my sister's best friend. You'd just

gotten out of a long-term relationship. I could see the other guys wanted you and I didn't want you to get hurt."

"Could it also be you wanted to protect yourself?"

"Maybe," he admits.

I rest my hand on his hard chest, aching to touch him some more. "You didn't want to want me. And you didn't want to have to fight the other guys for me. I understand."

"The second you walked through our door, I knew you'd be trouble. I thought the roommate contract would help, but I was a fool. In the end, I was the one who couldn't resist."

He tugs me back to him, wrapping my legs around his waist as he lifts me off the counter, fitting our bodies together as he kisses me desperately. I was right. Unlike Keith, I definitely wouldn't crush Shane. He holds me easily with nothing but his strong arms and hard body as his kiss sends sparks through me.

He sets me down reluctantly. "If you ever do want more, any one of us would be happy to give it to you. Obviously I want you to pick me, but I'll understand if you don't."

I swallow and nod. He gives me one last, smoldering look, before walking into his library. Leaving me all hot and bothered...and more confused than ever.

There's only one thing left to do, I guess: kiss Luke.

CHAPTER TWENTY-ONE

LUKE

I THROW open the door and toss my keys in the tray with a little more force than required. They bounce off and hit the floor, and I groan before picking them up. Today is seriously not my day, and tonight isn't getting any better. My best bet is to grab a beer, watch some football before bed, and try to forget today ever happened.

I head for my bedroom first, but stop in the doorway when I see someone is already in there.

Allie.

She sits on the edge of my bed and looks up at me nervously when I step inside. She jumps to her feet. "Luke. Um. I've been waiting for you."

"I see that." I close the door behind us and raise an eyebrow. "What are you doing in my room?"

"Your door was open and I thought..." She bites her lip. "It seems silly now. I shouldn't have come in here."

"It's fine. As you said, the door was open." I remove my

jacket and hang it up. "Honestly, walking in and seeing you on my bed is the best part of my day so far."

"What happened?" she asks, as she sits back on the bed.

"I had dinner with my agent. He's worried about my upcoming movie and says it better be a hit, or we're in trouble."

"What? You're a huge movie star! Sexiest man of the year and all that."

"I was. But after the Lana thing my career has been suffering."

"That's ridiculous! She's the one who looks bad, not you."

I sit beside Allie with a heavy sigh. "When Lana left me I did some stupid shit. Got wasted a lot. Trashed a hotel room. Slept with anything that moved. It wasn't pretty. The bad publicity is catching up to me now, I guess."

She rests a hand on my knee. "Your reaction to Lana's betrayal is totally understandable. And you're not doing any of that stuff anymore."

"True, but the press love to spin whatever they can to make me seem like a total wreck." I dig out the trashy tabloid my agent gave me at dinner and hand it to her. "Look at this shit."

Allie stares at the cover, which has a really unflattering picture of me in a baseball cap and sunglasses, my beard extra ragged that day, as I walk down the street with my head down. The headline reads, *Luke Hart's Drug Addiction – How He's Coping After Lana's Moved On To A New Man.*

"But that's not even true!" Allie says. "You're not on drugs. This is a complete lie."

"Welcome to life in Hollywood."

She tosses the tabloid aside. "No one reads this trash anyway. Everyone knows it's all totally fake."

"Someone reads it or they wouldn't keep selling it."

She sighs. "I wish I could do something to help."

I take her hand and bring it to my lips, kissing her palm. "You being here and listening to me is already helping."

"Good." She moves that hand to my jaw, running it across the rough stubble there, as she studies my face. I close my eyes and savor her touch. It's been ages since anyone caressed me like this. Yes, I fucked a lot of women after Lana, but those were quick and dirty encounters. This touch is intimate, almost loving.

I lean into it and then feel her other hand slide into my hair. God, it's good. Her soft touch. Her warm fingers stroking my face and head. Then her lips brush against mine and I can't keep in a soft groan.

She freezes at the sound and I open my eyes. She looks concerned, like she's not sure she should be doing this.

"Don't stop," I say.

Her fingers slide down to the back of my neck and she pulls my mouth to hers. At first we kiss slowly, brushing and nipping at each other's lips. Asking for permission to go further. We've both been hurt before and we both need to ease into this together. But there's no one I want to do this with more than Allie.

I start to take the kiss deeper, but instead she breaks off and gazes up at me. "Is this okay?" she asks.

"More than okay." I run my thumb along her sexy lips. "Allie, you're the only woman I've felt anything for since Lana."

Her eyes widen and I take that moment to draw her mouth back to mine. This time we're not tentative or hesitant or slow. This time I kiss her with all the passion I'm feeling and don't hold anything back. She melts in my arms and I wrap myself around her, holding her tight as I kiss her. Damn, I missed this. Just holding someone. Kissing them. Loving them.

Her soft lips trail down my jaw, along my stubble, to my neck. I groan and tilt my head back as she covers my skin with light kisses. At the same time, her fingers move to the front of my shirt and begin slowly undoing the buttons. Each bit of skin she reveals is covered with her mouth, and I get hard with the thought of her continuing even lower.

I'm not sure either of us is ready for that, though god knows I want it. I take her hands, stilling her movements as she opens the final button on my shirt, and drag her back up to my mouth. As I kiss her deeply, her hands splay across my chest, cool against my hot skin. I picture them wrapped around my dick and get even harder.

I run my fingers along her voluptuous thighs and hips. My previous lovers were all so skinny I worried I might snap them in two like a twig. I like that Allie has some meat on her bones and I'm dying to have her naked and wrapped around me.

And her breasts. Fuck, they're so hot. Large and perfectly shaped. I take them in my hands, feeling the nice weight of them while rubbing her hard nipples through the fabric of her dress. She moans and arches her back, and I increase the pressure.

I'm about to remove her dress and explore her body even more, when my door bangs open, startling us both.

"Hey, I—" my brother starts. His voice cuts off when he sees me with Allie, our hands all over each other.

Allie jumps to her feet, her face bright red. "Matt! I was just, um..." She glances between the two of us, biting her lip. "Oh god. I have to go."

Her face red, she dashes out of the room like the place is

on fire, leaving me alone with my brother. That total cock-blocker.

"Sorry, I didn't know she was with you," Matt says, looking at everything except me.

"It's okay." I begin buttoning my shirt again. The situation is awkward as hell, but what can we say? We all agreed to this. We all want her. And none of us is going to back down.

"What are we going to do about this mess?" Matt asks, gazing in the direction Allie ran. I know what he means. Soon one of us is going to have sex with her. Then what? We all take turns with her?

I shake my head. "No clue. But we better come up with a solution fast."

CHAPTER TWENTY-TWO

ALLIE

THE MUSIC PULSES around me as I raise my shot glass. "Bottoms up!"

Brooke arches an eyebrow as I down the tequila. It burns all the way down, but I shake it off. We've been in this club for the last hour and I still haven't forgotten the awkwardness from earlier today. Remembering Matt's startled face as he walked in on me with Luke gives me so much anxiety I can barely sit still. I was embarrassed, worried he was upset, but worst of all, incredibly turned on by the idea of Matt joining us. And maybe Shane too.

I have no idea how to get out of this mess I'm in. Alcohol is the only solution.

"What's going on with you?" Brooke asks. "I haven't seen you drink like this since spring break in our senior year."

My stomach turns at the memory. "Oh god, when I was so drunk I had sex with that guy in the pineapple costume." Not my finest moment.

"Yep. And then you had a killer hangover the next day."

She slides my empty shot glass away from me. "Better stop now or you'll have another one."

I slump against the bar counter, chin in hand. "Fine."

"Why don't you tell me what the problem is?"

"I did something stupid..." I hesitate, picking at a groove on the wooden counter.

Brooke taps her nails against her glass. Tonight they're a sexy dark red, for passion. Or maybe danger. "Spit it out then."

"I kissed all three guys."

She sits up straighter on her bar stool. "You did what now?"

"It's Shane's fault! He kissed me first."

Her jaw drops open. "My brother kissed you?"

"I know, I couldn't believe it either. I thought he hated me." I shake my head. "Then Matt and Luke walked in on us and kind of...demanded they get equal treatment."

She holds up a hand. "Wait a second. They forced you to kiss them?"

"No! It wasn't like that. They gave me the option to kiss them to make it even between all of us. So I did."

Brooke's mouth is grim. "And now you have feelings for all of them and don't know how you'll choose one."

"Yes! How'd you know?"

"Because this is exactly what I knew would happen if you moved in with them. Although I didn't expect you to go after all three of them." She raises her beer in salute. "Nice work there."

"I really need another drink." I wave down the bartender, then order a martini. Brooke doesn't stop me this time. She must realize what deep shit I'm in. "I know I can't have a relationship with all three guys, but I really like each of them. If I choose one, it'll cause problems with the others, who I still have to live with for another few weeks. How am I going to get out of this?"

She rests a hand on my arm. "Walk away now. Come live with me until you find your own place. Put all three guys out of your mind and consider it a post-breakup rebound fluke. Temporary insanity. It doesn't have to be anything more."

My chest tightens at the thought. "I can't do that."

"Why not?"

"Because I don't want to choose none of them either." I rest my head on my folded arms, hiding my face. "God, I'm a mess."

She rubs my back. "Well, there's one other option."

"What's that?" I ask, looking up with hopeful eyes.

"Convince the guys to all have a relationship with you."

My face scrunches up. "Is that a thing?"

"Sure. Polyamory."

"Like an open relationship? But I don't want them to sleep with anyone else. Oh my god, I'm so selfish."

"You are the least selfish person I know. It's nice to see you doing something for yourself for once."

I take a large gulp of my martini, which is not as good as the one Matt makes me, but it'll have to do. "The guys would never go for that. And how would I explain our relationship to other people?"

She shrugs. "It's none of their business anyway."

"You wouldn't judge me for having a relationship with all three guys?"

"Of course not. As far as I'm concerned, as long as people are happy and not hurting anyone they can do what they want. If you want a harem of men, go for it. The idea sounds disgusting to me, but if that's what tickles your fancy, do it."

I let out a sad laugh. "I suppose."

"Now a harem of women, on the other hand, that I could be down for. Remember when I was dating Tracy, Carmen, and Sheila all at once? They each knew about it." She flashes a smug smile. "That was my own little harem there."

"What happened in the end?"

"Um. Well." She takes a sip of her drink, not meeting my eyes. "It fell apart because each one wanted all of my time and attention. Originally they were okay with sharing me but then they got jealous and possessive and it turned ugly. In the end, we all broke up." She sighs. "Probably for the best. I can't even make time for one girlfriend at the moment. Work is seriously trying to kill me."

"I'm sorry." I perk up. "Hey, did you know Shane's co-star, the one who plays Jenna, is gay too?"

"Oh yeah? She's pretty hot."

"We should totally set you up!"

Brooke rolls her eyes. "Thanks but no thanks. Just because we're both gay doesn't mean we'll hit it off."

"Fine," I say. "But if you happen to come over and she's there too, well, what's the harm in that?"

"You're impossible. I don't set you up with every single straight guy I know."

"That's because you hate all of them other than your brother."

"Okay, you have a point there." She tilts her head as she stares at me. "So what are you going to do now?"

"I don't know." I chug the last of my drink. "For tonight, drown myself in alcohol."

"Not your best plan, but not your worst either."

"I just want to forget all of my relationship drama over the last month and drink and dance and have a good time."

She gestures for the bartender to fill up our drinks again. "We can definitely do all of that."

I grin and grab my martini, then head to the dance floor with her. Lights flash, music thumps, and I drink and dance and drink and dance. For the next few hours I lose myself in the steady pulse of the club and the people around me until I can barely stand up straight, and I'm leaning against Brooke while she pulls out her phone.

"Shane, I need you to come get me and Allie," she says, as I grip her arm tightly.

"No, don't call him!" I say, although my words are slurred. "Anyone but him."

"Too late. He's on his way."

"Why?" I ask, my head already pounding, the cool air only making it worse. Hang on. When did we go outside?

"Because he's the only one I trust."

I groan and rest my head back against the brick wall. Shane is the last person I want to see right now. The whole point of coming here was to forget about him and the other guys. But thanks to my best friend, this night is about to get a whole lot worse.

CHAPTER TWENTY-THREE

SHANE

I DROP everything and rush to the club the second Brooke calls me. She and I have always had a policy that if we needed the other to pick us up or rescue us from any situation, we'd do it—no questions asked.

Still, as my sister and her best friend climb into the backseat of my Tesla, both of them stumbling and muttering and reeking of alcohol, I have a *lot* of questions.

"You okay?" I ask, looking in the rearview mirror at them. I'm allowed at least that one.

Brooke nods. "Yeah. Just go."

Once they're buckled in, I stare forward at the road as I drive us back to my place. Now that I've seen how drunk both Brooke and Allie are, I'm really glad Brooke called me instead of getting a taxi or an Uber. With the state they're in, a driver could have easily taken advantage of them. Am I overprotective of my little sister? Definitely. And I'm fine with that.

What's more surprising is the fierce protectiveness I feel toward Allie as well. I told myself before it was just a kiss in the heat of the moment, that we had sexual chemistry and nothing else, but I was lying to myself. What I feel for her is more than lust...although there's a lot of that too.

The girls are unusually silent in the car, and when we get home I find that they're both passed out, leaning against each other. I bring Brooke in first and deposit her in the extra guest room, then head back out to get Allie. I lift her into my arms and she wakes up enough to snuggle against my chest as I carry her into the house and down the stairs to her room.

Allie wraps her arms around my neck as I help her onto the bed. "Shane," she whispers, as her fingers slide into my hair. "I want you. So bad."

Her mouth is clumsy as it finds mine and she tastes of alcohol, but I still can't resist her kiss. After a few seconds I pull away. I'm not taking advantage of a girl so drunk she won't remember any of this tomorrow.

"Don't go," she says, tugging on my shirt.

"Lie down," I say, as I extricate myself from her grip. "You need to rest. I'll get you some water."

When I turn to go, Matt and Luke hover in the doorway to her room, looking concerned. They must have heard us come in.

"Is she okay?" Luke asks.

Matt wrinkles his nose. "Wow, she smells like she went swimming in tequila."

"That's probably not far off," I say.

"Luke, Matt," Allie says, her eyes popping open.

They move to either side of the bed and gaze down at her. Luke strokes her face, while Matt takes her hand.

"Yes, Allie?" Luke asks.

"I'm sorry." Her face crumples up like she's going to cry.

"Why are you sorry?" Matt asks.

"Because I got us into this big mess."

Luke tucks a piece of red hair behind her ear. "Everything is going to be fine."

"No it's not." She sniffs. "I want all of you, but I can't have all of you. I have to choose. But I don't want to choose."

"Is *that* what this is about?" I ask, crossing my arms.

Luke nods slowly. "Matt walked in when Allie and I were kissing. She got upset and must have ran off to get drunk with Brooke."

"Thought I could forget." She squeezes her eyes closed. "Didn't work. Still want all of you."

I sigh and move to the end of the bed to take off her heels. "Don't worry about that tonight. Just get some rest."

Luke and Matt help ease her under the covers. She's still wearing her dress, but it would be weird to remove it when she's like this. None of us have that kind of relationship with her...yet.

"Can't. Don't want to lose any of you. Don't want to hurt any of you." She sighs. "Don't want to be alone."

"You're not alone," Matt says. "We're here with you."

"Brooke said I should talk to you guys," she mumbles, as she pulls the covers up to her chin. "About sharing."

"Sharing?" I ask, arching an eyebrow.

"Poly..." Her voice fades out. "Poly...something."

"Polyamory?" Luke asks.

"Yes!" She giggles. "My own personal harem of sexy actors."

"Technically that would be polyandry," I say, which makes Matt roll his eyes.

She giggles even more. "Yep. That's what I want. All three of you at once."

"Okay, now she's just babbling." Matt chuckles, then takes her hand and kisses it. "Go to sleep, Allie. In the morning I'll fix you up my favorite hangover cure."

"Yes, Matt." She closes her eyes again.

Luke kisses her on the forehead next, and then the three of us turn off the light and leave her in her room, closing the door behind us. Then we head upstairs to grab some beers.

"Well, shit," Luke says, as he pops open his beer. "What are we going to do?"

I shake my head. "We need to stop this thing with her right now. All of us. Enforce the roommate contract for real this time."

"Can you really do that?" Matt asks.

I frown and stare at my beer. "I don't know."

"I agree with Shane," Luke says. "There's no other option. She's tearing herself up over this. She'll never be happy picking only one of us, and even if she does, it will ruin our friendship with each other."

"There is one other option," Matt says slowly, glancing between us with a sly grin. "We do what she wants and agree to share her."

I nearly spit out my beer. "Seriously?"

"Why not?" Matt asks, with a casual shrug. "We all want her. She wants all of us. We could give it a try."

"No way! That's a crazy idea. There's no way it can end well."

"Matt may have a point," Luke says. "We're all best friends. We share a house. Why not try sharing her too?"

I can't believe Luke is on board with this idea too. "It will never work. We'll get jealous. Or possessive. Like you said, it'll destroy our friendship."

"Did you get jealous knowing she was kissing us?" Matt asks.

I open my mouth to answer, but then consider it. "No, actually. I suppose because we were open about it. It didn't feel like cheating."

Matt nods. "I wasn't jealous either, even when I walked in on her kissing my brother. I actually thought it was pretty hot."

"I think the answer's pretty clear," Luke says. "We either have to all agree to give her up...or all agree to share her."

We're quiet as we consider the situation and take sips of our beer. I don't want to give Allie up and neither do the other guys. But we've never shared a woman before. Can we really do it and avoid jealousy or other negative feelings? I'm not sure.

The strangest thing is...thinking of her with the other guys *is* actually kind of hot. Or even better, all three of us together. My dick twitches just imagining it. One of us in front, the other behind...

I finish off my beer and turn to the other guys. "Fine. Let's try it. But when this all goes to hell, don't say I didn't warn you."

CHAPTER TWENTY-FOUR

ALLIE

WHEN I WAKE UP, my head pounds like someone is jackhammering into it. Everything is too bright and too noisy and just *ow*. Damn you, tequila. And vodka. And whatever else I drank.

I'm still in my dress from last night, my hair is in tangles, and I seriously need a shower to rinse off the eau de alcohol clinging to me, but first I need to get rid of this massive headache. There's a glass of water by my side of the bed and I down the entire thing. Shane or one of the other guys must have left it there. I vaguely remember Shane picking me and Brooke up and the other two guys tucking me in and...oh.

Oh crap.

What did I say last night?

I rub my palms against my eyes, but it only makes the pain worse and does nothing to erase the memories of my stupid drunken ramblings last night. I can't believe I told them I wanted my own personal harem. I cringe again just thinking about it. No doubt they went and had a nice laugh at my expense afterward. Oh that Allie and the crazy things that come out of her mouth.

How am I supposed to face them ever again?

I get up to use the restroom, brush my teeth, and down a couple Advil, then take a quick shower before heading back to my room. Maybe if I hide in here until tomorrow they'll let me pretend last night didn't happen. Fat chance, but it's the only solution my hungover brain can come up with right now.

There's a light knock on my door and I groan. So much for hiding.

"Come in," I mutter.

All three of the guys stand outside my room. Seriously. All of them. I cannot catch a damn break. Don't they have something to do? Somewhere to be?

Guess not.

"Hey, Allie. How are you feeling?" Luke asks.

"Like shit."

"Of course you do," Matt says, as he walks over to me. He hands me a revolting-looking brown smoothie. "Drink this. I promise it'll make you feel a whole lot better."

I take a whiff and groan. "No way."

"It's disgusting but it works," Shane says. "We all can attest to Matt's hangover cure."

My head throbs and I sigh. "Fine."

Shane hands me an ice pack. "Put this on your forehead. It'll help the pain."

"And while you drink that, I'll give you a massage that should also help," Luke says.

"Thank you." They're being unusually nice and pampering. Maybe I freaked them out last night and they're worried I've gone off the deep end.

Luke moves behind me on the bed and begins rubbing my shoulders and back, while I press the ice pack to my forehead and drink this disgusting smoothie. The other two guys sit beside me on the bed in silence as Luke's fingers knead my muscles and convince my body to relax.

After a few minutes, my hangover loses its grip on me. I'm not sure if it's from Matt's magical drink, Shane's ice pack, Luke's talented fingers, or all of the above, but I'll take it.

"Thank you," I say. "I feel a lot better now."

"Anything else can we do for you?" Luke asks.

"Forget last night ever happened?"

"That's actually what we came to talk to you about," Shane says.

Oh crap. "I hope you didn't take anything I said seriously. I was really wasted and not thinking straight. It's best if you pretend it never happened."

"We can't do that," Matt says.

I draw in a deep breath. "Okay. I understand. Do you want me to move out?"

"No, of course not," Shane says, giving me a scowl. "Quite the opposite, in fact."

"What do you mean?"

"We want to try being in a relationship with you," Luke says.

"All of us," Matt adds.

My jaw practically hits the floor. "What now?"

Shane takes the melted ice pack from me. "None of us want to give you up, and we don't want to force you to choose. So now you don't have to."

I gape at the three of them. "And you're all on board with this?"

"I'm a bit skeptical it will work, but we're willing to try," Shane says. "For you."

"Wow." I sit back and glance between them, stunned into speechlessness. I never expected any of them to actually agree to this. It was a wild fantasy and nothing more. But somehow they're willing to try...for me. "What happens if it doesn't work?"

"I suspect it will destroy all of our friendships with each other," Shane says with a deep frown. "Let's make sure that doesn't happen."

"How about a test?" Matt asks. "We all kiss Allie now in front of each other. If we're too jealous or possessive, we end the experiment now. If not, we agree to continue with the plan."

"What do you think about that, Allie?" Luke asks.

Desire makes my pulse race. "I think that's a good idea."

"Then let's try it," Shane says.

Luke is closest to me and already has his hands on my body, so he pulls my hair to the side and begins kissing my neck. I face the other two guys, who watch the entire time as Luke trails kisses across my skin. Nervousness swirls through my stomach, but also desire and excitement too. A part of me is so scared of what will happen next, but another part of me likes the idea of them watching.

Luke turns my head toward him and captures my mouth with his. His lips are warm and firm as they take charge of the kiss, slowly deepening it and sliding his tongue inside. I rest a hand on his hard chest, feeling the strength underneath. I could kiss him all day long and this could easily turn into more, except I can't forget that the other two guys are there looking on.

I pull away from Luke and move from one brother to another. Matt draws me into his arms and our mouths find each other eagerly. There's something dirtier about his kiss, like a secret naughty promise as he swipes his tongue across my lips. His kiss is a tease, a hint of what else I could have from him later.

When he releases me, I turn to Shane. His eyes are dark and stormy with some strong emotion. Anger? Lust? Jealousy? I can't tell. He grabs my waist and yanks me toward him, kissing me hard and possessively, nibbling on my lower lip. He's rough and demanding but it only turns me on even more, especially when I remember the other guys are there too.

He lets me go and I touch my lips in wonder. I taste all three of them on my tongue still. I glance between the guys, eager to kiss them again. "How was that?"

"Really fucking hot," Matt says, with a naughty grin.

Relief and arousal flood me, because I feel the same way. But do the other guys?

"I actually liked it a lot," Luke says. "I wasn't jealous or anything. I just wanted to get in there too and join the fun."

Images of both him and his brother kissing me and putting their hands all over me flood my brain, making me press my thighs together. "Shane?" I ask.

"I didn't hate it," he reluctantly admits.

Matt nudges him. "He thought it was hot too."

Shane sniffs. "Maybe a little."

"The real test will be when we do more than kissing," Luke says.

"I, for one, am ready to get started on that," Matt says, winking at me.

My lady parts say hell yes, but my pounding head says hell

no. "Maybe when I'm not hungover. And what about, uh, diseases and stuff? We'll need a lot of condoms. Of course, I got tested after Parker and I'm on birth control, so maybe we don't need condoms after all..." Crap, I'm babbling again. I need to watch that.

Each guy stares at me with lust-filled eyes. Shane clears his throat. "I've been tested too."

"Same," Luke says.

"Oh yeah," Matt adds, licking his lips.

I relax against my pillow. "Great. One less thing to worry about."

Shane abruptly rises to his feet. "Let's give Allie a chance to rest and recover."

"And get out of here before we all jump her bones," Luke mutters.

"Just let us know if you need anything, okay?" Matt says, as he stands up.

"I will. Thanks." I give them all a warm smile. "For everything. The hangover help. Putting up with me last night. And now agreeing to try this, uh, whatever this is between us. I'm very lucky to have the three of you."

"We feel the same," Luke says.

Each one takes a turn placing a soft kiss on my lips before they exit the room, leaving me to wonder...did that really just happen?

CHAPTER TWENTY-FIVE

ALLIE

IT'S BEEN three days since my hangover-of-doom and the talk with the guys. They've all been busy with work, so I haven't seen them a ton since then, which is good because I'm still wrapping my head around this new joint relationship we're all in. How is this my life? I'm not complaining, but damn.

Every time I do see the guys, they're getting more comfortable kissing me. I know it won't be long before it turns into more, and desire flutters in my stomach at the thought. I think I'm finally ready.

I find Matt outside, lying in the sun on a lounge chair, wearing nothing but his swim trunks. His tanned, muscular chest and toned arms gleam under the sunlight and it's hard to look at anything else.

I toss a script in his lap. "Here you go."

His eyebrows dart up behind his sunglasses. "What's this?"

"I found the perfect script for you."

"Oh really." He picks it up and reads the title, then makes a face. "*Royal Screw-up?*"

"It's a romantic comedy about a prince who falls for a normal girl. It's funny and sexy and romantic and so perfect for you."

"A rom-com? Seriously?" He frowns and tosses the script aside. "*That's* what you picked?"

I pick the script off the ground and dust it off. "Trust me on this. All this time you've been going after parts like the ones your brother plays. Tough action heroes. Rugged cops. Superheroes who grunt a lot. But that's not you."

"It's not?" His face falls.

I rest my hand on his shoulder. "No, it's not. Those are Luke's roles, not yours. He's the strong protector type. But you? You're the sexy, funny guy that every girl wants."

"Of course I am," he says with a cocky smile. "But still, a rom-com? I don't know..."

"Matt, you need to stop trying to be your brother and play up to your own strengths. You're charming. Gorgeous. Clever. You're the perfect combo of naughty and nice. You're basically every girl's dream. That's why a movie like this is perfect for you."

"Hmm. All right. I'll read through it and check it out." He grabs my waist and pulls me down onto his lap on the lounge chair. "But right now I want to explore those things you just said. Am I this girl's dream too?"

I wrap my arms around his neck with a smile. "You know you are."

He presses his lips to the spot below my ear that drives me wild. "Maybe I can show you how very naughty and nice I can be."

I tilt my head to give him better access. "That's a good idea. But only if you agree to audition for this part."

He groans, but keeps kissing my neck. "All right. I'll do it, just for you. Happy now?"

"Yes." I run my hands down his firm chest, exploring the tanned muscles. He's so gorgeous it's almost painful to look at him, but I gladly suffer through it. I could stare at him forever. But it's not only the way he looks—it's everything about Matt. His heart, his humor, his flirty side. Even the amazing cocktails he makes me. Everything about him turns me on and makes me want him even more.

Our lips find each other and our kiss is hot and heavy. As his tongue slides against mine, he strokes my bare thighs and inches my dress higher, sending sparks of heat throughout my entire body. Excitement and desire sets me aflame and I spread my legs, inviting him to take this even further, and he gladly accepts. He finds my panties already soaked with desire and he flashes me a naughty grin.

"I think these need to go," he says, tugging at the fabric between my legs.

"Take them off then."

He drags my panties down my legs and tosses them to the ground, then slides his hands under my dress again, finding my bare, hot skin. The second he touches me, I sigh. It's been forever since anyone touched me there. Parker definitely neglected me for way too long. But dammit, I deserve better. I deserve a guy who treats me well and makes me feel this good all the time. Or maybe three of them.

"So wet," he says, as he rubs against my folds slowly. "You've been wanting this for a while, haven't you?"

"From the moment you opened the door that first day," I

admit. But then I moan as he continues to explore me with way too much patience. I'm so hot and ready for him I can't even think straight. "Matt, please."

He pulls my mouth back to his as his finger enters me. I kiss him hard as he plunges inside, giving me a taste of what I need from him. With his thumb he touches my clit, making me whimper into his mouth. My hips thrust toward him, wanting more and more. His talented fingers and lips fuel my passion, until all I can think about is getting us out of these clothes.

I grab the edge of his swim trunks and begin tugging at them. He chuckles at my eagerness, then helps me get them off him. I didn't think it was possible to be any more turned on than this, but the sight of him completely naked proves me wrong. He's glorious and thick and I want him inside me so badly I practically ache with longing. Every inch of Matt is mouth-watering and wow, there are a whole lot of inches on display right now.

He undoes the buttons on my dress and then lifts it off me, before tossing it aside. His eyes are hungry as he gazes down at my lace bra. As his mouth descends on my chest, kissing his way down my cleavage, his hands reach back to unclasp my bra. It falls off easily, revealing my large, full breasts and hard nipples. He cups them in each hand, then raises them to his lips to give each nipple a lick. My back arches, my head falling back as pleasure shoots through me.

I reach for his cock at the same time, circling my fingers around it to feel its thickness. It fills up my hand nicely and he's so much bigger than Parker was. Or any of my former boyfriends. Matt's reputation with the ladies definitely seems to be well-deserved so far.

"You ready for me?" he asks, as we stroke each other.

"Very ready."

"Thank god." He grabs my waist and pulls me closer so I straddle him. My knees are on either side of his hips on the lounge chair, our bodies lined up. We're both naked now, skin to skin, brimming with need for each other.

As his length presses against me, he looks me in the eye. "Am I the first one?"

I know what he means. The first one of the three roommates. "Yes, you are."

A wicked grin crosses his lips. "Good."

With that, he slowly slides inside me, directing me onto him with his hands on my hips. I gasp and press down to take more of him, practically begging for him to go faster, but he doesn't listen. He takes his time pushing inside me so I feel every single inch. He's so big it seems like it takes forever for him to fill me up, but I savor every second of it.

When he's all the way inside, he adjusts the lounge chair so it lays flat. Then he lies back and gazes up at me with a grin as I rise above him. "This view is incredible."

I slowly stroke my breasts. "I'm glad you like it."

He stares at my fingers as they circle my nipples. "Like it? I love it. I never want to look at anything else ever again."

"No?" I roll my hips once, taking him deeper. "I thought you were something of a player."

"Not anymore. Now I'm a one woman man." He grabs my waist with possessive fingers. "The only one I want is you, Allie."

A fluttery feeling fills my chest and I lean down to kiss him. Then I begin moving, slowly riding up and down on him, letting my breasts bounce above him. He watches eagerly, his eyes filled with lust, his fingers digging into my hips as he urges me on. Soon he begins to thrust up into me and together we find a steady rhythm that has us both gasping and moaning. I've wanted Matt from the first time we met and it's such a relief to finally have him—especially without any guilt about the other guys.

The sun beats down on us as we move together, neither one of us caring that the beach is only a few feet away or that any of the guys could get home, walk outside, and see us. Matt reaches up to fondle my breasts as I roll my hips faster and harder, plunging him deeper inside me. It's so good I don't want it to end, but I want to chase the feeling too, so I go faster and faster, building the incredible friction between us, until I can't hold on any longer.

With a loud moan the orgasm sweeps through me and makes me tighten up around Matt. My body is completely out of control as it bounces on him, wringing out every last bit of pleasure, until I feel him surge too. He groans and pulls me down to his chest as he releases himself inside me.

When the pleasure begins to fade, we both kiss as we try to catch our breaths and slow our racing hearts. His hands roam across my back and my ass, stroking me adoringly, while I rest on top of him. I slide my arms around his neck, loving the way it feels to be pressed against his strong body.

"You're the only woman I've been inside of without a condom," Matt says, between kisses. "That was amazing."

"It was." I brush my lips against his and roll my hips. I just had the most incredible sex of my life, and yet I already want more. He's made me insatiable. "We should do it again."

He groans and cups my ass, but that's when I notice we're not alone.

Shane watches from the doorway. I'm not sure how long

he's been standing there or how much he saw, but he doesn't look happy.

"Oh shit," Matt mutters, when he sees his friend standing there.

With Matt still inside me, I gaze into Shane's smoldering eyes. Something flares between us, before he turns away and storms inside.

I have to go after him.

CHAPTER TWENTY-SIX

ALLIE

I RELUCTANTLY STAND up as worry floods my stomach. Is Shane mad? Jealous? Did I ruin everything by sleeping with Matt? Is this new four-person relationship doomed to failure already?

I grab my dress off the ground. "I'm going to go talk to him."

"He'll be fine. Let him sulk. He knows the deal." Matt crosses his arms behind his head, still naked and looking so sexy I want to ride him again already. "Besides, that was worth it. I'm glad I got to be first."

"Yes, it was." I slide on my dress, then bend down to kiss him again. He grabs me and keeps me there longer, nipping at my lower lip, and it's hard to pull away from him. But eventually I do.

I chase after Shane, slipping inside the house. He's not in his bedroom, so I head up the stairs, calling out his name. I don't know what to expect when I find him. Will he give me his cold anger? His hot lust? Both?

I find Shane in his library, sitting behind his desk, feeding something into the shredder. He's wearing a dark suit, his dark blond hair shines in the sunlight, and his jaw is clenched and covered in the perfect amount of stubble. He looks so delicious I want to climb into his lap and kiss him roughly while yanking on his tie, hard.

I close the door behind me. "Shane, are you okay?"

"Fine," he says, his voice clipped.

I stand in front of his desk, but he won't look at me. Dammit. I knew getting into a relationship with three men would be complicated, but I didn't think it would backfire on us this quickly. "You don't seem fine. Are you upset because I slept with Matt?"

"No." He grabs another piece of paper to shred.

"Good, because this is what we all agreed to. Although if you want to back out now, I would understand." I lean forward, pressing my hands against his desk, showing off my cleavage. "But I really don't want you to back out."

He finally gives in and lets his piercing eyes linger on my breasts. I didn't bother putting a bra back on when I rushed to get dressed, nor my panties either for that matter. Shane's hot gaze takes it all in, as I wait to see what he will do next.

He rises to his full, tall height and stares down at me. I remain where I am, holding my breath as he moves around the desk and comes up behind me. Lust spreads through me at the feel of him brushing against me and the anticipation of what he will do next.

His hands unbutton the back of my dress and his mouth hovers near my neck, but doesn't touch me. Not yet. The dress falls to the floor and he stands back to admire my large ass, wide hips, and smooth back. There's no hiding my ample curves, but I don't try to cover myself or turn away. I let him look at me as much as he wants.

He moves close, the soft fabric of his suit pressing against my back, as I hear the unbuckling of his belt. My pulse races and desire sends heat between my legs as I wait for his next move. Shane and I have always had this intense love-hate chemistry, and right now my body is begging for him to take the next step.

"I wasn't mad," he says into my ear, before his teeth scrape against it. "Jealous maybe, because I wasn't the first. But mostly so turned on I couldn't see straight. I wanted to fuck you more than anything else in the world." His hard length rubs against my ass. "I still do."

"Do it," I beg, pressing my butt back against him, so excited I can't think of anything else except having him inside me. Every heated look, every passionate fight, and every forbidden kiss has led to this moment and now I practically thrum with need.

He bends me over the desk, pressing my hands flat against it, then nudges my legs wide apart. He grabs his cock in his fist before rubbing it against me, getting it nice and slick in both my juices and Matt's. The idea of having them both in one day is so dirty and so incredible, I nearly come again just thinking about it.

Without warning, Shane pushes into me, hard. He thrusts deep, filling me up, and oh god is he long and big. So big I feel completely stuffed as he begins moving into me from behind. He doesn't give me a second to adjust or catch my breath, he starts pounding into me. And damn, it feels good. Somehow it's exactly what I needed.

He reaches around to grab my breasts, yanking me back

against him, pushing even deeper inside me. All I can do is cry out and succumb to his rough, demanding thrusts as he holds me in place with possessive hands. His mouth finds my neck, and he claims my entire body as his.

"You're mine," his voice whispers near my ear. "Say it."

"Yours," I gasp, as he fills me up again.

"That's right."

Then he pulls out of me completely.

I whimper, but then he rubs himself between my cheeks. I gasp at the new sensation, especially as his thickness brushes my tight hole. I can't help but press back against him, wanting more of it.

"Has anyone taken you here?" he asks.

I swallow. "No. Never."

"I'll be the first then."

He moves to the other side of his desk, giving me a view of his incredible cock, which juts out of his open trousers. I can only watch and tremble as he opens a drawer and pulls out something. A small container. Then he moves behind me again and opens the cap. I hear the sound of him rubbing something slick all over his shaft, then his finger touches my back entrance.

"Ohh," I moan, as he pushes his finger inside. The stretching feeling isn't exactly painful, but it's new and unexpected. No man has ever touched me there before and I'm a little nervous it might hurt. Still, I trust Shane to take good care of me. He's been looking out for me the entire time I've lived here, even if I didn't realize it before. Plus, if one finger feels this good, I can only imagine how his entire length will feel.

He slides another slippery finger inside and thrusts in and

out, stretching me wide. I moan and push back against him, and just when I'm getting used to it, his fingers slip out.

"I think you're ready for me now," Shane says.

I cry out as he slowly enters me back there, and he goes still until my body adjusts to his size. "More," I gasp out.

He moves deeper inside me and I moan so loud I'm sure everyone in all of Malibu hears me. It's incredible, this mix of pleasure and pain, this amazing torture. I've never experienced anything like it before.

"That's it," he says. "Relax and let me in."

I will my muscles to relax and it does get easier for him to enter me. He feels gigantic like this and I don't think I'll be able to take him completely, but then somehow he's all the way inside, his hips flush against me.

"You're so tight," Shane says, his voice hoarse. "Your ass is incredible."

He begins to move then, sliding out of me slowly, before slamming back in fast, and the pleasure heightens tenfold. With even strokes he continues his beautiful torment and I push my hips back at him to take him deeper. I never knew this could feel so good. I was always afraid to try, but now I never want it to end.

When I think it can't get any better, Shane's hand slips around to thrust two fingers into me. At the same time, he begins rubbing my clit with his thumb in a way that's just right. He's possessed my entire body, truly making me his and his alone in this moment. Being touched in so many places at once by him is too much for me, and I grab onto the edge of the table and practically howl, trembling as the climax crashes into me hard. Shane holds me tight as I fall apart, overwhelmed by the amazing pleasure lighting up every nerve in my body. It keeps going on and on as he increases his speed, before he finally lets my name tumble from his lips and gives himself over to me completely.

He bends us both over the desk, his still-dressed body pressed against my back. He threads his fingers through mine over our heads in a way that is somehow both tender and dominant and so very Shane.

"You're remarkable," he says, pressing a kiss to my neck. "And so fucking sexy."

"Am I?" I ask, my voice flirty but tired.

He squeezes my butt cheek as he pulls out of me. "You know you are. One sight of your ass and I knew I had to make it mine."

I stand up and turn to lean against his desk, mainly so I can look at him again. He's so deliciously disheveled with his slacks open, his hair messy, and his eyes filled with just-sated desire. "I never knew it would feel so good."

He arches an eyebrow. "Does that mean you want to do it again sometime?"

"Definitely." I grab his tie and pull him closer. "And a dozen other things too."

A sinful smile crosses his lips. "We'll do all of them. Every single one."

CHAPTER TWENTY-SEVEN

ALLIE

I WRAP the towel around myself and poke my head out of the bathroom, checking to make sure none of the guys are around. All clear.

Of course, there's no reason to do that anymore. Two of the guys have seen me naked and been inside me. I don't need to sneak around inside this house ever again. The thought makes me almost giddy.

I slip inside my bedroom and toss my towel on the bed, then grab my brush. Except as soon as I touch it, I spot a *giant* spider on the wall right next to my closet. And I do mean humongous. I know, I know, spiders are my weakness, but seriously, this one is definitely a poisonous beast intent on murdering me in my sleep.

Okay, I tell myself, taking a deep breath. Don't panic. You are an adult. You can totally handle this. You don't need to call one of the guys to help you. They'll just tease you again.

After my little pep talk, I grab a tissue. This is it. I'm going in.

As I reach for the giant sucker, it *moves*. All those long legs coming right for me. I drop the tissue, scream, and jump on the bed.

Great, now I'm trapped. The beady-eyed little bastard is holding me hostage. I'm totally naked, but I can't get to my closet and I can't leave the room either.

I have to yell for the guys. That's the only option. Except I'm not sure if the guys are even here. They might all be at work.

Crap.

Maybe I can handle it by myself after all. I glance at the spider again and shudder. Nope, nope, nope.

Swallowing my pride, I send the guys a group text. None of them seem to have heard my screaming, but maybe one of them is in the house after all.

Help! I text them.

What is it? Luke writes back immediately.

Spider emergency!

I raise my phone and snap a pic of the massive spider so they understand how serious this situation is, then immediately send it off. Yes, they're going to tease me about it, but whatever. Maybe one of them will come deal with it for me.

I grab my towel off the bed and wrap it around myself, then bite my lip as I wait. Where are the guys? Surely one of them must be home? Maybe they can't see the spider in the pic? I click on the photo to check...and nearly drop my phone. Because I didn't just get a picture of the spider, but of the mirror to the right of it. And in that mirror?

Me.

Totally butt naked.

And I'm not talking a classy ass shot here. Oh no, this is

full frontal nudity. Boobs, hoohaa, the whole shebang. All on glorious display in my photo. It's the female equivalent of a dick pic.

And I sent it to all three guys.

Kill me now.

I fall onto the bed, covering my face with my pillow. I've never been so mortified in my life. Yes, some of them have seen me naked before, but not like this. How am I supposed to face them now?

Maybe they won't see it. Yeah. They'll just look at that spider and that's it. Totally.

Shit. I'm doomed.

It's decided then, I have to move out. No, that's not enough. I need to change my name. Flee the country. Fake my death.

Except they'll still have the photo. Even if I make them delete it, it's not exactly something you can un-see. Let's face it. Naked people are like a car crash. You have to look.

A knock sounds on my door.

I dash back and forth in the small space, first to the door, then to my closet to grab something to cover up with, until I remember the spider is still there and I can't get to my closet, then back to the door. I wrap the towel tightly around myself, smooth my hair, and stand as straight as possible. Then I open the door.

Luke stands outside it with his arms crossed. His eyes dip down, taking in the towel and lingering a little longer on my bare skin. I swallow. Yep. He definitely saw more than just the spider.

"Need help with something?" he asks.

My cheeks are on fire, but I try to act normal as I point toward the closet. "There's a spider holding my clothes hostage. Can you get rid of it for me? Please?"

A slow, cocky smile slides across his lips. The kind of smile I've seen in gifs of him before. "You sure there's a spider? Or did you want to lure me here with that glimpse of you naked?"

"I don't know what you're talking about."

"Uh huh." He strolls over to my closet and eyes the spot where the spider was. "I don't see anything."

"Oh god. He's hiding now. He's waiting until I fall asleep and then he's going to get me."

"Pretty sure he's not." He turns back to me. "But you can always sleep in my room if you're worried."

"That picture I sent was an accident. I didn't realize I was in it. Obviously. Can you forget you even saw it?"

"Not likely." He cocks his head. "Would it make you feel better if you saw me naked too?"

"I've seen you naked. In like three different movies."

He grins. "Not *all* of me."

I tug the towel tighter. "Well, there was also that sex tape of you and Lana, but I heard it's a fake."

"It's not."

My eyes widen. "Oh."

He grips the hem of his shirt and tugs it off his chest, flashing me with his tanned skin and hard muscles. I gape at him. "What are you doing?"

"Making us even." He reaches for his jeans and pops the button open.

"You don't need to do that. It's fine. Really!"

But he doesn't listen, and before I can process what's

happening, he slides those jeans to the floor. He's wearing nothing underneath. Totally commando. And holy crap, he has the biggest cock I've ever seen and it's not even erect. Except as I stare at it, that begins to change. As if he's getting turned on by the idea of me gawking at his naked body.

I've seen him nearly naked in movies, but he's even better in person. He's so ripped he doesn't look real and I want to run my fingers over his abs to convince myself I'm not dreaming.

"There," he says, grinning at me. "Now we're even."

I swallow and slowly nod. He's rendered me completely speechless with his glorious, muscular body.

He rests his hands on my waist, over the towel, and gazes into my eyes. "You don't need to be embarrassed, you know. You're gorgeous."

"Thanks." I tentatively reach out and press my palm to his chest. It's so firm underneath my fingertips. "You're pretty amazing yourself."

He steps even closer and the only thing between us is this tiny little towel that barely covers me, which I'm seriously tempted to toss aside. Even after sleeping with Shane and Matt yesterday I'm still so damn horny I can barely stand it, and having this Greek god of a man naked in front of me is only making it worse.

But then I spot something black moving behind him. The spider!

"There it is!" I gasp and point, and Luke spins around. He grabs a tissue and squashes the monster, giving me a view of his firm ass at the same time.

"Happy now?" he asks, after he disposes of the beast and turns back to me.

"Very." I slide my arms around his neck. "My hero."
"Does that mean I get a reward?"
"Definitely. Anything you want."
He looks down at me and slowly grins. "I want you."

CHAPTER TWENTY-EIGHT

LUKE

MY LIPS CRASH DOWN on hers and she lets out a little sigh, like she's as relieved as I am. Her hands are all over me, exploring my body as I kiss her deeper, and I want to do the same to her. I tug at the edge of her towel, dragging it off her, revealing her damp naked skin. I pull away from the kiss so I can look down at her. God damn she is sexy. All those lush curves I want to dig my fingers into. Those large breasts that beg me to take them into my mouth. Those voluptuous thighs I can't wait to spread wide.

"You're beautiful," I tell her, as I pull her close again, flush against my chest, her breasts pressed against me.

"You're not so bad yourself," she murmurs, as she nips at my lips.

Her slick body rubs against mine and I'm so hard it's almost painful. I want to go slow, to go down on her, to make this last, but I also need her bad. And from the way she wraps a leg around me, her hips pressing against mine so I rub right between her thighs, I get the feeling she wants me inside her immediately too.

I reach down to grasp her full, round ass, which fits perfectly in my hands. Then I lift her up, wrapping her legs around my waist.

"I'm sorry," I tell her, as my cock slides against her wet pussy, trying to ease its way inside. "I can't go slow. Not this time."

"I don't want slow," she says, her arms tight around my neck. "I want you to take me. Hard and fast. Right now."

Her words elicit a hungry growl from me, as I grip her hips and nudge against her entrance. With one hard push I'm inside, all the way to the hilt, and we both moan. She's so tight and feels so good around me, for a second all I can do is simply hold her there in my arms, her entire body wrapped around me, sheathing me with her warmth. I bury my face in her neck, overcome with unexpected emotion. She's not the first woman I've slept with since my divorce, but she's the first woman I've slept with that I've cared about.

When I don't move, she begins to roll her hips, riding up and down slowly on me. My arms strain to hold her, and I push her against the wall hard enough to get a gasp out of her. With her back pressed to the wall I can lift her higher, getting exactly the right leverage to begin thrusting in and out of her at the perfect angle to make her moan. I can tell it's good for her because she throws her head back and lets me take control as I pump in and out of her.

"You like that?" I ask, as I thrust deep into her.

"God yes. Don't stop, Luke."

"I won't. Not until you come for me."

I place my hands flat against the wall on either side of her head and stare into her eyes as I keep pounding her. She clings to me tightly with her arms and legs and I never want her to let go. I want to be inside her forever just like this.

"Oh god," she moans, her eyes rolling back.

I move harder and faster, slamming her back against the wall, and the little cries she makes only urge me on. Then she practically screams my name, her fingernails digging into my shoulders, as she tightens up around me. I almost come right then too, but I hold off. I want this to last. I want to make her come again.

When she finishes trembling, I spin us around and put her down on the edge of her bed. I stand right in front of her, then I grab those sexy legs and lift them up, so her ankles rest on my shoulders. This gives me the perfect view of her full breasts, which I cup in my hands as I fondle her pebbled nipples.

Then I begin sliding into her again with long, deep strokes. Delaying my own pleasure, but slowly building hers up again. Her fingers dig into the sheets, gripping them tight, as her moans get louder and louder again. I can tell she's getting close, and I grab her legs with one hand to hold her tight as I pound into her, while finding her clit with my other hand. Right as I begin rubbing her she comes again, hands fisting the sheets, eyes closed, and the look on her face is so hot I lose myself too, coming hot and fast inside her.

"Fuck," I gasp out, as I nearly fall on top of her. She wraps her legs around me again as I press a soft kiss to her neck.

"That was amazing," she says. "You made me come twice."

"Not enough if you ask me. Next time I'll go slower. I just couldn't help myself."

"Me either." She runs a hand through my hair lazily as I

relax on top of her. "Are you okay with this arrangement we have? After what happened with your wife…"

I push myself up on my arms to look at her face. "With us all sleeping with you? Yeah, surprisingly I am. Maybe because we're all being open about it. What Lana did was totally different. She went behind my back. But this doesn't feel like cheating."

"Good." She pulls me close for a kiss. "If any of you were uncomfortable with this, I'd stop it. But as long as you're all okay with it, I'm going to keep enjoying the benefits."

"Is that so?" Her kiss is already getting me excited again, making me hard while still inside her. Jesus, I'm like a horny teenager all over again when she's around. "Because we could try out some more of those benefits now."

"I'd like that."

"Me too. But before we do that, there's something I need to ask you for help with."

"Anything."

"The premiere for my movie is next week. Will you go with me?"

Her eyes widen and a smile lights up her face, making her somehow even more beautiful. "I'd love to."

CHAPTER TWENTY-NINE

ALLIE

"EARTH TO ALLIE," Kristen says, waving a hand in front of my face. "You okay there?"

I quickly sit up straight at the receptionist's desk. "Sorry, just daydreaming." AKA thinking about my three guys naked, along with all the things they did to me. It's been hard to think about anything else lately. They've turned me into total mush.

I'm filling in at my sister's vet office again, and we're currently in a rare moment of quiet between appointments. Kristen's hair is strawberry blond and currently done up in a perfect bun on her head. Her vet coat is impeccably clean and well-pressed, along with her gray sheath dress and professional black heels. Everything about her is in stark contrast to my wild red hair that refuses to be tamed and my blue retro dress with a stain on the boob from the curry I had at lunch.

"I recognize that look," Kristen says with a smile. "It's the one you get when you have a crush on someone."

"Oh, it's more than a crush," I mutter as I focus on organizing the charts in front of me.

"Ooh really? Who is he? Spill!" She perches on the edge of my desk, her eyes dancing with excitement. Kristen's been married to a great guy ever since she graduated college and they have two cute kids together, but she always enjoys hearing about my love life.

"Well, um, I'm sort of dating three guys at once," I blurt out before I think better of it.

Her jaw falls open. "No way. In secret?"

I stack the charts again awkwardly, not meeting her eyes. I should not have told her about this. Why did I even bring it up? "No, they all know about each other."

"Seriously?" Her jaw practically touches the floor now, but then she recovers. "Wait, is this some kind of Tinder hook-up culture thing? I think I read an article about that online."

I bite out a laugh. "No, it's not like that. It wasn't anything we planned, but we're all living together and it just kind of happened. It was their idea actually."

"Wow. That sounds complicated. And pretty hot. But how is that going to work out long-term? Will you pick one eventually?"

"I don't know. I'm trying to just enjoy it at the moment and see what happens. I have feelings for all of them, so I'd like to keep seeing them as long as I can."

Kristen's expression turn concerned. "What about marriage though? Don't you want to get married someday?"

My chest tightens. "I do, but..."

"And what about mom and dad? They'd totally freak if they knew about this. So would your school, I bet. Would they let you keep teaching there if it got out?"

I sigh. Leave it to Kristen to bring up all the practical realities I've been trying not to think about in my post-sex haze.

She's right, of course, but I still hate hearing it. Now there's a huge knot of anxiety in my stomach at the thought of my parents or anyone at school finding out. People would never understand this strange and wonderful relationship I'm in with Shane, Luke, and Matt. And since I'm dating three guys who are constantly in the spotlight, someone is going to find out sooner or later.

"I'm still trying to figure it all out," I say. "And I will eventually. Can you please be happy for me in the meantime?"

"I am happy for you. I just want you to think this through also." She squeezes my arm. "I love you and only want the best for you. But I'm your big sister and have to look out for you too. That's my job, after all."

I know she only means well, but now she's put all these doubts and fears in my head. Reminders that there is no way the world will ever accept this relationship. What happens when people find out? Our careers could be destroyed. Our families might never speak to us again. Could the four of us survive that?

And what about marriage? I've always dreamed of getting married in a big ceremony with all my family and friends watching, but there's no way I can marry three guys. Am I giving up on that dream too by being with them?

When I get off work I head to the mall to meet Brooke, hoping she can ease my worries. If anyone can make me feel better, it's her.

"You slept with *all three of them?*" Brooke asks, way too loudly. Other people turn and look at us and I duck my head, my cheeks burning.

"Yes, but you don't need to tell everyone in the mall about it."

"Sorry, I'm just...wow. Damn. I need to wrap my head around this. While trying not to picture you and my brother together, because ew."

I bite my lip and glance at my best friend. "Do you think I'm a slut?"

She turns toward me, her face serious. "No. *No*. Definitely not. I think you're my fucking hero."

I laugh, relieved. "You don't even like guys though."

"Nope, but I'm still impressed. You go girl!"

I shake my head with a rueful smile. "I can't believe you just said that."

She grins as she scans the clothing racks in front of us. "If there's ever a time for it, it's when your best friend bangs three of the most eligible bachelors in the world like a damn queen. I never thought this harem idea of yours would actually work, but I'm really happy for you."

"Thanks. We'll see if it actually works though. So far the guys are okay with it, but I worry they'll change their minds or get jealous or decide they don't want to share anymore."

"I get that. Three guys and one girl is definitely a tricky situation. Especially three actors who are used to getting what they want. I think the best thing you can do is enjoy this while it lasts."

"But what will happen when people find out about my relationship with the guys? What will they think? You might not think I'm a slut, but other people will."

She rests her hands on my shoulders, giving me a serious look. "Who cares what they think? You have to do what makes you happy. I learned that when I came out to my parents and the people in my office. Some people were okay with it. Some weren't. I say, fuck 'em. If they can't accept us for who we are and who we love, they don't deserve a second of our time anyway."

I nod. I know she's right, but I also know the guys and I will all be miserable if our entire world falls apart because of what we're doing.

I turn back to the racks and pull out a short black dress. "What about this?"

"Hot. Definitely try it on."

We're at the mall shopping for me for once. Not that I'm rolling in dough or anything, but Luke gave me his credit card and told me to buy the most expensive dress I could find, along with shoes, a purse, and anything else I needed for his movie premiere. At first I felt bad, but then he reminded me that I'm doing him a favor by going with him. He doesn't want to go alone, especially with his agent pressuring him to make sure this movie does well. Eventually I agreed to spend his money, mainly because I don't have a dress that would work for this event, and I really need to look good. Especially since the media will be all over me and Luke being there together.

"Wait," Brooke says, pulling a hanger off the rack. "I found it. This is the perfect dress to complement your red hair."

She holds up a beautiful emerald green gown that normally I'd be too shy to wear because it's both sexy and expensive. But for this event I'm going all out.

I take the dress from her. "I'll try it."

We grab a couple more, then I head into the dressing room while Brooke waits outside. The first couple dresses emphasize my curves in all the wrong ways. The black dress I picked looks good on me though. I step outside and let Brooke check it out.

"Love it. Your body looks great, but it's very safe. Go try on the green one. Trust me on this. I'm an expert on women's bodies, after all." She winks as I slip back inside the dressing room.

I put the black dress in the maybe section, then put on the green one Brooke picked out. As soon as it's on, I gasp when I see myself in the mirror. It's so much more daring than anything I'd usually wear, but it makes my hair and skin really pop and shows off my breasts and narrow waist, while emphasizing my wide hips. I look like a voluptuous sex goddess.

I step out of the dressing room and Brooke lets out a low whistle. "Damn, girl. That dress is smoking hot on you."

I run my hands down the smooth fabric. "You don't think it's too much?"

"No, I think it's perfect. Never take it off. Unless you're getting naked with someone, of course. And after the guys see you in that dress, they won't be able to take their hands off you."

I laugh and slip back inside the dressing room, then study myself in the mirror. My cheeks are flushed, my hair is a little wild, and the gown hugs my body in all the right ways. I look like a woman who's ready to get ravished. Luke is going to love it. So will the other guys, for that matter.

I put back the safe black dress and get the green one. Time to be a little bold.

As we head to the shoe section, I say, "Enough about my love life. What's going on with yours?"

"A big fat nothing. Which is how I want it."

"Uh huh."

"What?"

"You say that, but then I see you picking up women whenever you can."

"Sure, for a little bit of fun. I don't have time for anything more than that."

"I bet you would if you found the right woman."

She nudges me with her hip. "Ah, but since you're taken now, I'm out of luck." She holds up a pair of red peep-toe heels. "How about these?"

"Love them." Shopping with Brooke is way more fun now that I can actually spend money. Plus, she's always had the best taste in clothing, even if she saves the colors for me and for her nails. Today they're a shimmery gold, like she dipped her fingertips in a bowl of glitter.

But she's changing the subject on purpose. I elbow her. "We'll find you someone. Don't worry."

"I'm fine. Seeing you happy is all I need, I promise. And it doesn't hurt that my brother is happy too."

For now anyway, I silently add. But what happens when things stop being new and fun, and reality sets in?

CHAPTER THIRTY

MATT

EXCITEMENT COURSES through me as I race through the house. I need to find Allie and tell her the good news. She's going to be thrilled, and I can't wait to see the smile on her face.

I check her room, but she's not in there, although I hear the shower going in the bathroom next to it. I ease open the door a tiny bit. "Allie? You in here?"

Allie gasps. "Matt!"

I grin and step inside the bathroom. The shower walls are glass, giving me a perfect view of Allie's curvy, wet, and very naked body. She looks so hot with her red hair hanging around her shoulders and her skin flushed with heat. "Mmm, best thing I've seen all day."

"What are you doing in here?"

I completely forget whatever I was originally doing as desire for Allie makes my dick instantly hard. I yank off my shirt and toss it on the floor. "Thought I might join you in there."

"But...I'm naked!"

I laugh. "I've seen you naked before. Shit, you sent me a naked photo of yourself the other day."

"That was an accident."

I pause in the middle of unbuttoning my jeans and look up to see her watching me. "I can go, if you'd rather I not join you."

She licks her lips in an enticing way. "No, you're definitely welcome in here. The shower's plenty big for the two of us."

"I was hoping you'd say that." I slide off my jeans and boxer briefs, then open the shower door and slip inside. Steam instantly surrounds me and I wrap my hands around Allie's waist, moving close to give her a long, thorough kiss that has her clinging to me. My hands roam her body, her skin slippery from the water, while our lips and tongues dance and seduce each other.

"I got some good news today," I say, as I cup her breasts. I love the way they feel in my hands. So full and heavy, filling up my palms. The perfect size for my fingers to caress.

She rests her palms on my chest as she begins licking the water off my neck. "Oh yeah?"

I tilt my head, closing my eyes as she kisses along my jaw. "I got that part in the romantic comedy you picked out."

"Really?" She lets out an excited little squee and pulls back to smile at me. "I'm so happy for you!"

That bright smile makes the victory that much better. I draw her into my arms, pressing her body against mine. "Like you predicted, they thought I was perfect for the role."

She playfully swats at me. "Told you so."

"Yes, you did. I'll have to get you to help me with other scripts in the future."

"Any time. It was actually really fun reading them all and imagining you playing the characters."

"And now I think you deserve a reward for helping me get my next role." I bend down and lick drops off her breasts, flicking my tongue against her hard nipples.

She throws her head back and her hand wanders down to my cock at the same time, giving it a squeeze that makes me groan. "Me? I didn't do anything. You deserve a reward for nailing the audition."

As she begins stroking me, I ask, "How about we both celebrate together then?"

"I like the sound of that."

I shove her back against the tile wall, spread her legs, and slide my hand between her thighs. She's already soaking wet, and not just from the shower. My fingers run along her slit, teasing her, but then I have a better idea. I lower myself to my knees, hooking one leg over my shoulder, and find her pussy with my tongue.

She gasps as I taste her, while the shower sprays water against my back. She's so sweet I immediately want more. I plunge my tongue inside her, slowly loving her with my mouth. Her fingers tangle in my hair, holding my head as I suck and lick her. I listen to her gasps and feel the way her thighs quiver and her fingers tighten in my hair until I know exactly the right pressure and speed to drive her wild. Soon she's crying out and moving her hips wildly and then she comes into my mouth with a glorious shout. One orgasm down. I wonder how many more I can give her in here?

"Oh my god," she says, her head back against the tile, her eyes sultry and satisfied. I raise myself to my feet again and kiss her hard, letting her taste herself on my tongue.

"We're just getting started," I tell her.

Then I spin her around so her breasts and hands are flat against the tile, and rub my length against her from behind. Damn, she has a great ass. I grab one of her cheeks in one hand as I slowly slide inside her.

"Matt," she moans, as I fill her up. It feels as amazing as it did the first time we had sex. I wonder if it will ever be anything less with her? Somehow I doubt it. I've never felt this way about any other girl before, and god knows I've been with a ton of them. But that was just sex. This is a lot more.

Once I'm sheathed inside her, I press one hand flat on her stomach and guide her hips into a slow, rolling rhythm, almost as if we're dancing together. Our bodies rock back and forth, wet skin sliding against wet skin, keeping me buried deep inside her the entire time.

With my other hand I begin slowly rubbing her clit. She pushes her hips back at me, taking me deeper, and we move as one, our bodies in tandem, fitting together like we were made for each other. I wonder if the other guys feel this way too when they're inside her. Do they also think she's their perfect match? Or is it just me?

Thinking about her having sex with the other guys only turns me on more, even though it should probably make me jealous. I never imagined I'd share a woman with them, but if I had to do it with anyone, at least it's with my best friend and my brother. We're playing with fire though. This situation will either tear us apart forever—or bind us together even tighter.

"More," Allie begs.

"You want more of this?" I ask, pulling almost entirely out of her. When she whimpers, I slam back into her, hard.

"Yes! Yes!" she cries out, as the orgasm makes her legs

tremble and her body contract around me. She yells my name, and I'm sure if any of the guys are home they must hear her crying out. I like the idea of that.

My suspicions are confirmed when the bathroom door opens a minute later. "What are you two doing in here?" Luke asks.

"What's it look like?" I ask, as he steps inside, watching me pump into Allie from behind.

"Taking good care of her, from the sounds she was making."

It turns me on even more, having my brother watch, and Allie seems to like it too. She turns her head toward him with lust in her eyes and calls out, "Want to join us?"

Holy shit. I nearly come right then at the thought. It's so damn wrong, but the idea of my brother joining us and pleasing her at the same time also sounds so damn right.

"I think I will," Luke says.

He tears off his clothes and his dick is already hard and straining to get inside her. He steps into the shower and I pull out of Allie, knowing if I stay another second I'll lose my load, and I want to make this last.

Allie turns toward Luke and wraps her arms around him, kissing him hard. They devour each other's mouths, while I rinse off under the water. It's seriously hot, especially as their hands stroke each other. She grabs his cock, he grabs her ass, and more than anything, I want to see him sliding inside her. Then I want to join in too.

Both of us inside her at the same time... It's a fantasy I always had but was too afraid to admit to anyone.

Now I can actually live it.

CHAPTER THIRTY-ONE

ALLIE

I PULL AWAY from Luke's very sexy mouth and glance back at Matt standing under the water. His face is dark, his eyes tight, and I realize I didn't ask him if he was okay with his brother joining us. I made the decision without checking with him first, and now he looks upset. Or maybe excited. I can't tell.

I rest one hand on Luke's chest and the other on Matt's. "Are you both okay with this?"

"You know I am," Luke says.

"Definitely," Matt says. "I want to see him fuck you."

My eyes widen at that. "You do?"

"Yeah." He pushes me gently back toward his brother. "And then I want to join in too."

"What do you think of that?" Luke asks, as he pulls me against his hard, powerful body. "Both of us inside you at once?"

"It sounds amazing." Desire floods me at the thought. I don't care what anyone might think of us anymore. All I know is I've never wanted anything more in my entire life...except for a foursome with Shane too. Only he could make this even better. Maybe next time, although I'm not sure Shane would ever go for something like that.

"Let's make it happen then," Matt says, as he moves behind me and begins kissing my shoulders.

Together the brothers run their hands all over my body, worshipping me like a goddess. Their mouths cover me too, from my lips to my neck to my breasts. Every inch of me feels adored and loved. All I can do is relax and let them take me on this journey with them.

Luke picks me up and wraps my legs around his waist, like he did the other day. I hold onto his broad shoulders, enjoying the feel of his hard, wet body pressed against my breasts. Without warning, he thrusts inside, making me gasp as he fills me up.

"God, that's so hot," Matt says, as his hands cup my ass. He grabs hold of it and makes my hips rock back and forth, moving me up and down on his brother.

Luke leans back against the wall with a groan. "Yes, just like that."

Matt moves in closer, his length pressed between my cheeks, as he grips my waist and urges me to move faster. My slippery wet body slides between both men, and all I want is more and more.

Then I feel Matt's fingers stroke between my cheeks, finding my tight hole. "Shane told me he took you here the other day," he says, in my ear.

"He told you?" I ask, surprised. I didn't realize the guys talked about having sex with me.

"Oh yeah. Bragged all about how he was the first. Lucky guy." He slides one finger inside and I moan.

"Do you want to be the second?" I ask.

"Fuck yes," Matt says, as his finger stretches me out. "Do you think you can handle us both?"

My hips jerk at the thought, both with lust and hesitation. They're both so big, but I want to try. "Yes. I want both of you."

"You heard the lady," Luke says. "Let's give her what she wants."

"My pleasure," Matt says, as his finger leaves my back entrance and is replaced by the slippery head of his cock. I'm so turned on I'm ready for anything.

I cling to Luke's shoulders, gasping as Matt fills me up inch by inch. Luke captures my mouth, distracting me with his kiss while holding me tight. Matt takes his time, waiting for my body to adjust, and the slight pain begins to give way to pleasure. By the time he's fully sheathed, I'm moaning into Luke's mouth and begging for more.

Both brothers inside me at the same time, pressing me tight between their muscular, wet bodies? I'm in heaven.

And it only gets better once they start moving. There's no way to describe the exquisite feel of both of them sliding in and out of me at the same time with long, deep strokes that have my toes curling and my nerves tingling. Thank god they're both holding me up, because my entire body has gone weak with the pleasure flooding me. All I can do is give myself over to them completely and let them take me away to paradise.

"How's that feel?" Luke asks me.

"So good," I manage to get out. "Oh god, don't stop."

"Trust me, we won't," Matt says.

They find the perfect rhythm, rocking me back and forth between them, our bodies rolling and grinding and moving as one while the shower sprays hot water down on us. I've never felt so deliciously full before, or so loved and cherished. Both brothers have complete control over my body, claiming it as their own, yet they're sharing me too. I belong to both of them, and it means everything to me that they're both okay with that. No, more than okay. They both seem to find it as amazing as I do.

Somehow Matt's fingers find their way to my clit, and he begins rubbing it while they continue their dual thrusts. I cry out as the pleasure intensifies, and the guys begin moving faster. Ramming into me in front and in back, plunging deep inside, while Luke begins stroking my nipples. It's too much and my cries turn to whimpers as every one of my nerves tingles.

"Oh god." My nails dig into Luke's shoulders, and my head rests back against Matt's shoulder. "Luke...Matt..."

"That's it, Allie," Matt says.

"Come for us, baby," Luke adds.

With a yell, the climax rushes through me, making me tighten up on both of them, which only makes it feel even better. They don't stop, just keep going through all of my shuddering moans, supporting my body as they milk every drop of pleasure from me. Only then do they both let themselves go as well, coming at the same time inside of me with simultaneous groans.

For a few minutes all we can do is cling to one another as the trembling fades and the warm water washes over us. I'm so weak I don't think I can walk or even stand, but wow, it was so worth it.

Once we've recovered, Luke lowers me to my feet, Matt shuts off the water, and somehow we stumble out of the shower and into my bedroom. We collapse on the bed, all of us still dripping wet, and I lie back with one guy on either side of me. They both wrap their arms around me, snuggling close, tangling their limbs with mine. I kiss Matt and then Luke, resting a hand on each brother possessively. *Mine.*

"Jesus," Matt says. "That was incredible."

"It really was," Luke agrees.

"The best thing I've ever felt in my life," I say. "I only wish Shane could join us too."

Matt snorts. "Fat chance of that ever happening."

I sigh. "Oh well, a girl can dream."

CHAPTER THIRTY-TWO

SHANE

"THIS IS MY TRAILER, where I spend most of my time between takes," I say, as I open the door for Allie.

"Ooh," she says, as she steps up into it and glances around. "Very dark and masculine. It's so you."

I chuckle softly. "I suppose so."

She makes her way to the leather seats and sinks down onto them. "Thanks for giving me a tour. I've never been on the set of a TV show before."

"Of course." I move to the mini fridge and grab us some bottled water. "There wouldn't even be a show anymore if not for your genius idea."

"I'm so excited the producers went for it," she says, as she takes the water with a smile. "Then they turned Diana into a villain, which was truly genius. The fans are going to go wild once the show airs."

I nod as I sink beside her on the couch. "Nadia loves being a villain too. She can put her hatred of me to good use that way, I suppose. She's asked the writers to kill her off at the end of the season too, and she's already looking for something new." I slide an arm around Allie's waist and pull her close. "It all worked out, thanks to you."

"All I did was suggest that Jenna and Talon would be perfect for each other." She shrugs. "Seems obvious to me. You and Nadia always had bad chemistry."

"Yes, we really did. Probably because she meant nothing to me. I didn't feel anything for her. Not like I do with you."

Allie's eyes widen and then she blurts out, "Shane, I slept with both Luke and Matt."

"I know. You've slept with all of us. We agreed to that." I run a hand through her long, red hair, thinking about how it'd look wrapped around my fist. "I may not like it, but..."

"No, I mean together. At the same time. In the shower." She covers her face in her hands.

"Oh. I see." For a few seconds I imagine it. Both of the brothers surrounding her behind the glass walls of the shower. It's oddly arousing, even though I'm jealous too. Although I can't tell if I'm jealous because they got to have her together... or because I wasn't there to join in.

She bites her lip. "Is that okay? I realize now we never discussed that sort of thing."

"We never laid out any real terms or conditions, so you're welcome to do whatever you want."

Her shoulders relax. "I suppose you should have made a new roommate contract to cover this."

"Probably. But we'll figure this out as we go. None of us have done this before." I tilt my head and study her. "Did you enjoy it? Both of them at once?"

"God, yes. It was the most incredible experience of my life. I only wish..." She looks away and hesitates.

"Wish what?"

"Wish you'd been there too."

The idea excites me more than I like, but it sets off a lot of red flags too. I frown. "I agreed to be in this relationship with you and the other guys. I'm trying to be fine with that, even with you sleeping with them in my own house. But watching you with other guys? Sharing you in the same bed? I'm not sure I can do that."

"I understand," she says, but I can hear the disappointment in her voice.

"I'll consider it, okay?" I slide my hand under her skirt. "But when you're with me, you're mine and mine alone."

She nods, passion flaring in her eyes. "I'm yours."

I grab the back of her head and draw her toward me, taking her mouth hard with all my pent-up lust. But then the trailer door bangs open and a voice lets out a little shriek.

We break apart as Hannah says, "I'm so sorry. I'll come back later."

I sigh, but the mood has already been ruined. "It's fine. I want you to meet Allie anyway."

Hannah steps inside the trailer and shuts the door. "I heard you're the one to thank for saving our show and coming up with the new romance angle."

Allie gives Hannah one of her radiant smiles. "I didn't do much, really."

"Well, I thank you either way. Even if I have to kiss this guy now for the camera." She makes a sour face.

Allie laughs. "Have you met Shane's sister? I think you'd get along."

"Ugh," I say, at the thought of my friend and my sister

together. I wonder if that's how Brooke feels about me and Allie.

"Nope," Hannah says. "But if she's got his blond hair and smoldering eyes I'm all for it."

"She totally does," Allie says. "We'll have to introduce you sometime."

"I'd like that." Hannah gives me a wry smile as she heads for the door. "I'll leave you two alone now. But filming starts again in ten minutes, so make it a quick one." With a little wave, she shuts the door behind her.

Allie turns back to me, resting her hands on my shoulders. "Where were we?"

I glance at the nearby clock and sigh. "I was about to kiss you senseless and then have my way with you on the couch, but I have to get back on set, unfortunately. Break time is over."

Her eyes widen with excitement. "Can I come watch? I like seeing you do all those fight scenes. And who knew you were so good at parkour?"

"Of course you can. As long as you can withstand Nadia's death glare, that is."

Allie shrugs. "She doesn't scare me. Besides, I'm the one who won you over in the end."

I pull her in for another kiss. "That you did."

CHAPTER THIRTY-THREE

ALLIE

I TRUDGE BACK to my Ford Focus at a slug's pace. It's my first day back at work and I forgot how totally exhausting teaching high school kids is. And I'm supposed to make it through another year of this? Don't get me wrong, I love it, I really do. But damn.

God, I really hope my car turns on. Another warning light popped up on the clunker's dashboard this morning, which is the absolute last thing I need right now. As soon as my first paycheck from this semester comes through, I'll take it in to get checked out. Promise.

As I fumble for my keys, I hear a man's voice say, "Hey, Allie."

I jump, gripping my keys tight as I spin around to face whoever has approached me in an empty parking lot. But then I loosen my fingers when I see who it is and the fear is replaced by annoyance. "Parker? What are you doing here?"

His dark hair is perfectly styled and his face clean-shaven. He's wearing a gray suit, so I guess he came straight from the office. "I need to talk to you, but I don't know where you live now and you weren't returning my calls."

I cross my arms. "So you thought you'd show up at the place where I work out of the blue?"

"Don't be like that. I know I messed up." He steps forward. "But I want you back, Allie."

I gape at him. "Seriously?"

"Amy and I didn't work out, and I realized you're the one I love anyway. I should have asked you to marry me after all. We were perfect together."

"No, we *seemed* perfect together, but we really weren't. Then you went and started banging someone else behind my back."

He presses his lips together tightly and starts again. "That was a mistake. I realize I'll need to rebuild your trust, but I swear I won't cheat on you again. I promise."

Wow, this guy has some nerve. I honestly can't believe he thinks I'd get back together with him. Even if I wasn't with my three sexy actors now, I wouldn't date Parker again for anything. In fact, I'm starting to question what I ever saw in him at all.

I shake my head. "I will never take you back. Not in a million years."

He rests his hand on my arm. "Please, give me a chance."

I shake him off and step back. "No way. Besides, I've already moved on."

His jaw drops. "What? Already?"

"Yep. And I'm much happier than I ever was with you. I realize now that you and I were just not meant to be."

"That's bullshit. Who are you with?" His eyes narrow. "Let me guess, one of your new roommates?"

"Yes," I say, which isn't technically a lie. I'm definitely with one of them. And also two more. But I have no desire to explain our complicated relationship to my stupid ex, and it's none of his business anyway. I just want to get away from him so I can go home to see the guys who actually treat me well.

He scoffs. "You have to know that'll never work out. They're actors, for one thing. They could get any girl they want and pretty soon they'll get bored of you and find someone else."

I grab my keys and turn toward my car. "Thanks for your opinion that no one asked for."

"C'mon Allie. You're doing the same thing you did with me. Living with the guy you're dating. Falling for him way too fast. Putting the pressure on. Is it any wonder I ran to another woman?"

I grip my keys so hard they dig into my skin. "I never want to see your face or hear your voice again, Parker. We are done. Stay out of my life. Got it?"

"I can't do that. I love you, Allie. I won't let you go."

Something in his voice sends a chill down my spine. Or maybe it's the possessive way he's staring at me. "You don't have a choice. I'm already gone. Now please, leave me alone."

I get in my car and slam the door shut before he can say another word. Then I speed out of the parking lot with screeching tires, anxious to get away from him and his creepy words. I always thought Parker was a decent guy, but now I'm worried I was wrong about him. Either way, I have a feeling that won't be the last of him.

Besides, he has no idea what he's talking about. Not only is he a jealous, cheating slimeball, but he's simply wrong about my relationship with Shane, Luke, and Matt. What we have together is real, I know it. Yes, I fell for them quickly, and yes, we all live together, but it works. For now, anyway.

I can't help but worry it's all going to come crashing down soon though. Luke's movie premiere is tomorrow night and people will photograph us together. What if it gets out I'm dating the other guys too? Everything could fall apart and the entire world will be watching. I picture Parker's smug face. I hear Kristen saying, "I told you so." I imagine all the phone calls and strange looks and coworkers who'll no longer talk to me. Not to mention, what it might do to the guys' careers.

But there's only one way out of this mess, and I'm not ready to end things with the guys. I'm happy for the first time in ages and what I feel for each of them is a hundred times stronger than what I felt for Parker. The idea of losing them makes my heart clench. No, that's not an option. All we can do is keep moving forward and hope for the best.

CHAPTER THIRTY-FOUR

LUKE

I PACE BACK AND FORTH, my nerves twitching under my skin. It's the night of my movie premiere and the pressure is intense. Everyone will be watching to see if I've recovered from my divorce, and my entire career is riding on this movie doing well. The one bright spot is that Allie will be by my side.

She arrives at the top of the stairs and I forget about everything else, because she looks stunning in a tight green gown that makes her red hair stand out even more. It's cut low and hugs her body and I can't decide if I want to keep staring or rip it off her and take her right now. Or maybe leave the dress on as I take her...

"You're going to be the most gorgeous woman there," I say, as I take her hand. "No one will even look at anyone else."

"Thank you," she says, her cheeks blushing.

"No, thank you for agreeing to come with me."

"It's my pleasure, especially when you're dressed like that." She tugs on my tuxedo jacket with a flirty grin.

I lead her outside, where a black limo awaits us. The driver opens the door and Allie slides inside, a big smile on her face. I climb in after her, then wrap an arm around her shoulders.

"Fancy," Allie says, her eyes wide as she takes in the leather seats, silver accents, and low mood lighting. "I've never been in a limo before."

As the driver begins to take us to our destination, I open the tiny fridge and pour us a glass of champagne. "Better get used to it. You're dating three actors now."

She shakes her head as she takes the glass from me. "It's still hard to believe sometimes. Most of you seem so down-to-earth most of the time. Then you do stuff like this and remind me how out of my league you really are."

"Hey." I rest a hand on her knee and gaze into her eyes. "We're not out of your league. Don't ever think that. In fact, one of the reasons I like you is because you're not impressed by the glitz and glam of Hollywood. Unlike many of the other women I've dated, you don't want me because I'm rich and famous, or because you think I could benefit your career by being photographed with me." I take her hand and a press a kiss to it. "You're real, Allie. And in this business that is a rare and beautiful thing."

"Thanks." She brushes back a piece of her wayward hair. "Sorry. I'm nervous about tonight, I guess. This is all new for me and so outside of my normal, everyday life."

"I understand. I was just a country boy from a small town before I came to Los Angeles. It took me a while to adjust to this lifestyle too. But you don't need to worry at all. You're perfect."

"Okay, I'll try not to stress." She takes a long sip of her champagne, finishing the entire glass.

"Maybe I can help." I set my glass down and turn toward her. Her makeup and hair took lots of work, so I know she'll be upset if I mess them up before we arrive. Instead I sink to my knees in front of her on the floor of the limo and push her low gown up, then begin spreading her legs wide.

"What are you doing?" she asks.

"Helping you relax." I begin kissing the inside arch of her knees. "Just lie back and enjoy the ride."

"Mmm, I can do that," she says, as my lips trail up her thighs.

I hook my fingers on the edge of her panties before looking up into her green eyes. They're full of lust and anticipation and she watches as I slide the tiny black thong off her. Oh yeah, she definitely planned for some action tonight when she put that on. I wonder if her bra matches it.

"I've been dying to taste you for ages," I say, as I push the dress up to her hips.

She leans back against the leather seat and spreads her legs wide, giving me better access as I move between her thighs.

I kiss my way up to her mound and then slowly lick at her folds, taking my time to thoroughly tease her sensitive skin. She's delicious and I can't stop myself from sliding my tongue inside her to get a better taste. Damn, she's so wet already. I would love to shove my cock inside and have my way with her, but right now this is all about her. Nothing will relax her more than me taking good care of her needs.

I stroke her with my tongue for a minute, listening to her soft moans, before working my way up to her clit. She gasps as my lips surround it and begin sucking. Then I add in my tongue too and her hips lift up to bury my face even deeper. I wrap her legs around my shoulders and cup her ass in my hands to lift her up toward my mouth, like an offering. Except I'm the one who's going to worship her.

I eat her out nice and slow at first, but then pick up my pace as she begs for more, her fingers tangling in my hair and pressing my face down. Her cries only get louder as I slip a finger inside her. I bet the limo driver has a pretty good idea what's going on back here.

"Luke," she says, between moans. "Yes, just like that."

I thrust another finger into her in response, while at the same time flicking her with my tongue. That gets a loud moan and a hip thrust, and I can tell she's getting close. I pump my fingers in and out of her faster, taking control of her pleasure with my mouth and hands. She's mine tonight and I want to taste it when she comes for me.

When she climaxes, it's beautiful. Her pussy clenches up around my fingers. Her back arches off the seat. A loud moan escapes her lips. And she clings to my head so I don't pull away or stop. I keep going down on her and making the orgasm go on and on as long as I can, until she's practically begging me to stop because it's too intense. Only then do I let her go and sit back to look at her face.

She has that beautiful post-orgasm face I've seen before and want to see every day of my life. "Wow. Thank you."

"Feeling better?" I ask, while I use a napkin to clean us both off.

"Much."

She reaches for her panties, but I stop her and stuff the thong in my pocket. "No, I want to know you're naked under there. That I can take you at any time in a dark corner. Or slip my hand under your dress and touch you." I grin as I caress her thigh. "If I get bored during the movie I'm doing exactly that."

"Promise?"

Before I can answer, the limo pulls up at the theater and we're instantly surrounded by the crowd of fans and paparazzi. Allie sucks in a breath as we look through the tinted windows at the red carpet that awaits us.

I take her hand. "Ready?"

She squeezes it. "Yes. But are you?"

I glance back out there, at everyone who will be watching tonight, and nod. "With you at my side, yes."

The driver opens the door and I step out first and give everyone a quick wave. The onlookers shout and cheer and snap photos, but I turn back and reach down to help Allie from the car. She steps out gracefully and moves to my side, staring at the crowd as cameras flash and people yell my name. She must be completely overwhelmed, but all she does is gaze up at me with her bright smile and my nerves settle.

We take a step forward down the red carpet and are immediately assaulted by the press, who thrust microphones in our faces. I keep walking, ignoring the questions about who Allie is, but keep smiling too. Posing for photos. Waving at the crowd. It's all a big show, but Allie handles herself amazingly well.

I do too, until another limo pulls up and my ex-wife gets out. What is Lana doing here? She's not even in this movie. Someone must have invited her to get a reaction out of me. Something for the press to focus on for the next few months. But as Lana steps out of the limo and meets my gaze, I feel absolutely nothing for the first time ever. Not love. Not bitterness. Not rage. Just...nothing.

And it's all because of Allie. She's helped me move on and she's the only woman here I care about.

I give Lana a quick nod and then slide my arm around Allie's waist. "Let's go watch a movie."

CHAPTER THIRTY-FIVE

ALLIE

"BEST NIGHT EVER," I say as we step through the front door and into the house. Luke walks in behind me and my chest feels all bubbly, as if I've just drunk an entire bottle of champagne. Tonight was perfect—from the limo, to the red carpet, to the movie itself—and I know I'll never forget it. Nor the man I spent it with.

"You were amazing," Luke says as his hands slide around my waist.

"Your movie was amazing," I reply, before pulling him in for a deep kiss.

Matt walks in then, wearing only his swim trunks and glistening with water. He heads for the fridge, grabs a beer, then cracks it open and watches the two of us kiss. When we pull apart, he grins.

"Don't stop because of me," he says. "How'd it go tonight?"

"It was great," Luke says.

"Except for Lana being there," I add.

"No, that was great too. I saw her and felt nothing." Luke's fingers stroke my back idly. "The only woman I cared about was already at my side."

"Good to hear," Matt says. "Why don't you two join us at the pool? We're taking a midnight swim."

"I'd love to," I say, unable to resist the idea of seeing Matt and Shane half-naked and in the pool.

Luke and I follow Matt down the steps and through the sliding door leading to the patio. Shane is in the pool already, and as we approach, he surfaces and I'm hit by a wave of lust as I watch the water rippling off his powerful body.

"You look gorgeous," he says, eyeing my gown.

"Thank you."

"Good enough to eat," Matt says, as he leans down and gives me a kiss, tugging on my lower lip with his teeth. I laugh and push him away playfully.

"I think it's about time you joined us in the pool," he says.

"With both of you?" I ask, glancing at Shane. "I need to take care of Luke first though. I owe him for earlier."

"No, go ahead," Luke says, as he lays back on the lounge chair, still in his mouth-wateringly sexy tuxedo. "I want to watch you...swim."

I turn back to Matt and run a hand down my tight green dress with a sly smile. "But I don't have a bathing suit."

"Trust me, you won't need one." Matt turns me around and slowly unzips the back of my gown, letting his hands caress me as it slides down my body to the floor. The other two men watch, their eyes glued to me as I stand in front of them in only a black lace bra.

"No panties?" Shane asks, his voice husky.

Luke pulls them out of his tuxedo pocket with a cocky grin. "I took them from her earlier."

"Sounds like someone's already had some fun tonight," Matt says, as he unclasps my bra and frees my breasts. Before I would have been nervous about being naked in front of them like this, but not anymore. The three of them have given me so much more confidence since moving in with them, and I know they want me exactly the way I am.

Luke puts his hands behind his head as he leans back on the chair. "I got her nice and ready for you. She tastes divine, by the way."

"I bet she does," Shane says.

Matt stands behind me and cups my breasts in his hands, slowly rubbing my nipples until they grow hard under his fingers. He tilts me so both of the other men can see us as he caresses me. I throw back my head, leaning it against his shoulder, as his touches send heat throughout my core. While Shane and Luke watch, his fingers slide down my skin slowly, drawing their eyes to my breasts, then my stomach, then my hips, before moving between my legs. He strokes me there as I wrap my arms around his neck behind me, clinging to him as he gets me wet and excited. When he slips that finger inside me, Shane lets out a soft groan, like he's in pain.

"Get in the water," Matt says into my ear, his voice low so only I can hear it. "Go to Shane. I want to watch you screw him."

I turn toward Matt, placing my hands on his bare chest as I whisper, "Shane said he didn't want to do that with you two around."

"He's lying. He wants us to watch too." He shrugs slightly. "But if that's really how he feels, he can leave."

I nod, filled with desire at the thought of taking turns with each of my men. I want to be bound to the three of them in a way we've never been before, with nothing between us. No secrets. No jealousies. No worries or fears. Just lust…and maybe something even more than that.

I pull away from Matt's expert hands with some reluctance, then slowly step into the pool, my eyes locked on Shane. As I sink into the water, letting it cover my naked skin and creep over my breasts, his eyes burn with need.

"Shane," I say, as I move toward him. "Is it okay if I join you in here?"

"Definitely." He glides through the water and then grabs me, crushing me against his chest before kissing me hard. His muscular, wet body presses against my breasts and all I want is to feel more of him against me, inside me, everywhere. I run my hands down his firm back, then push down his swim trunks, grabbing a handful of his tight ass.

"I want this," I whisper to him, as his tongue licks water off my neck. "But I understand if you want to stop too. We can go somewhere alone, or…"

In response, he lets out a primal growl and yanks his swim trunks off. He tosses them out of the pool, while Matt and Luke both let out loud cheers. Shane's hard length nudges at my hip under the water and my eyes widen while my heart pounds faster. We're really doing this then.

From this moment on, there's no going back.

CHAPTER THIRTY-SIX

ALLIE

"GET OVER HERE," Shane says, pulling me tight against him.

I slide my arms around his neck, playing with the wet hair at his nape, and then wrap my legs around his waist. Fitting us together in the water, where we can float as one. I stare into Shane's eyes, my pulse racing, as emotion flickers in my chest. I never thought he'd want to do this, or that he'd be okay with this arrangement we all have, but he is. He's willing to do this for me. And that means everything.

When he slides inside me, I glance over my shoulder at Matt and Luke, wanting to see their reactions. Luke is still watching from the lounge chair with a hungry expression, while Matt now perches on the side of the pool with his legs in the water, his eyes eager. They both look like they're enjoying this as much as Shane and I are, which only turns me on more.

Shane clasps me tight against him when he's fully sheathed inside me. "God, you feel so good," he says. "I love your body so much."

Warmth spreads through me at his words and I kiss him passionately as he begins to move. Shane is rock hard and the feel of him sliding between my folds is exquisite. His large hands run up and down my back as his mouth devours mine, joining us together in every way.

Sex is so easy and fluid in the water, our bodies finding a natural rhythm together, creating waves as we get closer to release. His thrusts are long and steady, hitting me deep as I cling to his shoulders. My legs tighten around him and I arch back into the water, letting it lap over my naked body, while he takes me higher and higher.

He holds my hips tight and picks up the pace, with the water flowing around us. Little moans escape me as he hits me in exactly the right angle, over and over, until I can't help but come apart. My core clenches up around him and I hold onto his body as if I might get swept away if I let go. He growls again, surging inside me, before he loses control. His mouth slants across mine and he steals one last, possessive kiss as the orgasms rock through us together.

He pulls back and stares into my eyes. But before he releases me, he says, "Matt. Take her."

Matt's in the water a second later, and I feel his naked body at my back, his hands skimming along my skin. He lifts me away from Shane, and I'm too dazed from my receding orgasm to do anything except wrap my arms and legs around him now. As Shane's length leaves me, Matt's pushes inside, immediately filling me up again.

"Yes," I moan, as I move from one lover to another.

"Told you he wanted to watch," Matt says, into my ear.

Shane leaves his hands on my body while Matt begins thrusting up into me. Matt's rougher and faster than Shane was tonight, probably from being so turned on while watching me screw his best friend. And to my surprise, Shane doesn't leave. Instead he squeezes my ass and kisses my neck, which only makes the experience even better.

"Harder," I tell Matt, as I dig my fingers into his back, feeling that friction building between us. It won't be long before he brings me to my second orgasm at this pace.

"You heard her," Shane says.

"If that's what you want," Matt says, as he thrusts deep into me.

"I want it all," I say.

I turn my head back to capture Shane's lips, and catch sight of Luke outside the pool. He's opened his tuxedo pants and now grips his cock in his hand, giving it long, slow strokes while he observes us. I let out a little moan at the sight.

Matt grabs the edge of the pool, using it to get more leverage as he pounds into me and sends choppy waves across the water. Shane slides his hand between our bodies, finding my clit and rubbing me in exactly the right way to make me gasp. I throw my head back and let out a loud cry as the orgasm claims me, rocking through my entire body. As the pleasure ripples throughout me, Matt thrust deep and fills me with his warm release.

His forehead presses against mine, while Shane wraps his arms around us both. For a moment the three of us simply hold each other, breathing in and out as one.

My body is so limp now from all the orgasms, but I'm not finished yet.

"Take me to your brother," I tell Matt, once I can speak.

Matt and Shane gently pick me up and lift me out of the water, carrying me to Luke's arms like I'm a precious gift. Luke seats me on his lap, making me straddle him, and enters me easily. I cling to his broad shoulders and pull his mouth to mine, his tuxedo brushing up against my breasts.

"I want to see you come again with me inside you," Luke says, as he begins thrusting up into me, his large hands circling my waist.

"I don't know if I can," I say, although I'm already feeling that nerve-tingling rush building up again.

"Sure you can," Matt says. His talented fingers stroke my thighs and slide between my legs, quickly making me see stars. At the same time, Shane's hands begin roaming across my breasts, working their magic on my already-sensitive nipples.

All three of them are touching me now, their six hands demanding more from my body than I can handle. But there's no stopping this now, and I don't want to stop either. All I can do is let my desires take over and succumb to the pleasure as I ride Luke and lean into Matt and Shane's strokes. When they each begin kissing my neck, my back, and my lips, I'm totally lost. I fall apart completely, surrendering to the delicious release, dragging Luke with me into a toe-curling orgasm.

I kiss Luke softly as the last throes of pleasure grip us, then turn to kiss Shane and Matt too. I stroke their faces tenderly, amazed they were willing to share this moment with me tonight. They hold me tight, surrounding me with their love, like none of them ever wants to let go.

We pull apart reluctantly, then slip into the pool and float together with content smiles on our faces. Whatever happens between us now, I'll never forget this experience and how they made me feel—like I was the most special woman in the world.

CHAPTER THIRTY-SEVEN

ALLIE

AFTER ANOTHER LONG, grueling day at work teaching high school kids about *The Scarlet Letter* and *The Great Gatsby*, I want nothing more than to drop my bags on my bed, head to the beach, and drown myself in a good romance novel. Or maybe act one out, if one of the guys is around. Or all three of them.

But when I step inside the house I can tell something is wrong.

Luke, Matt, and Shane stand around the kitchen island and there's a tense feeling surrounding all of them. They glare at each other, arms crossed, shoulders stiff. Like I walked in on the tail end of a fight.

"What's going on?" I ask as I set down my bag.

"Here," Shane says, picking up a magazine and handing it to me. "See for yourself."

It's a tabloid and it has a picture of me and Luke on the cover, taken at the premiere. They got a very unflattering picture of me in which my green dress has turned me from a sex goddess to a lumpy sausage. My face is also all red and splotchy. Beside us, the headline says, *Luke Hart's Rebound Woman—Has He Finally Moved On?*

"Oh god, is that how I looked that night?" I ask, covering my mouth.

"No, not even close," Matt says.

"You were gorgeous," Luke adds. "They Photoshop it to make us both look worse."

"I don't know, you still look pretty good." Then again, it would be impossible to make Luke look bad in a tuxedo.

I flip open the article and there are better pictures of me inside, including one from my work ID photo. Creepy—how did they get that? They know way too much about me, but a lot of what they say is either untrue or pure speculation.

"Well, it could be a lot worse," I say, as I close it up.

"It's all over the internet too," Shane says, his voice sharp. "Now the entire world thinks you're Luke's girlfriend."

I glance between them as worry begins to eat away at me, along with everything my sister said. "Is that bad? Am I not his girlfriend?"

"You are," Matt says. "But you're our girlfriend as well."

Shane scowls. "Except now the press knows you're with Luke, so if you're seen with any of us, it'll be a disaster."

"Exactly," Luke says. "We can't let it be known that we're all dating you. It'll kill our careers."

Matt glares at his brother. "Maybe you should have thought about that before you paraded her around at your movie premiere."

"You're right," I say. "We can't let anyone find out about this. So what do we do?"

"There's only one option," Luke says. "You act as my girlfriend for the press and hide your relationship with the other guys."

"That's bullshit," Shane growls. "Besides, everyone on the set of *Talon* knows she is dating me."

"Yeah, why do you get to claim her?" Matt asks, standing up a little taller as he faces his brother.

"You have another solution?" Luke asks.

Matt rubs his stubbled jaw as he considers. "What if we each date her and are vague about it with the press? They can speculate as much as they want and we'll deal with the fallout later, if there is any."

The other guys are silent as they consider his words. Luke's brow is furrowed in thought, probably worried about his reputation. He just recovered it after his messy divorce with Lana and is on the rise again, but this could kill his momentum. Shane crosses his arms and stares at the countertops, likely worried about his show getting cancelled. Matt must be concerned about his new movie role too, since his career is finally getting back on track.

"All right," Shane says. "We'll keep our private life as private as we can. If the press asks, we'll be vague. They'll say whatever they want anyway."

"Will that work?" I ask, biting my lip.

"For a while, at least," Luke says. "And if they do find out, we'll deal with it together."

Anxiety makes my stomach churn. "How?"

Luke bows his head. "I don't know."

"Hey, we'll get through this," Matt says, wrapping an arm around my shoulder. "I promise."

But I'm not so easily reassured. "Aren't you worried what will happen if people find out about us? Not just the media, but our families? Coworkers? Friends?" I shake my head. "Once the news is out, things will never be the same. It could tear us apart and ruin all of our careers."

"I worry about that too," Shane says, as he takes my hand. "I'm sure we all do. But we're not going to let those concerns stop us from living our lives the way we want."

"Besides, this is Los Angeles," Matt says with a wink. "Anything goes here, right?"

"Maybe..." I say, but I can't summon much enthusiasm.

The guys share a look, then lead me over to the white couch in the living room and sit down on it. Shane is in the middle, and he pulls me onto his lap, with Luke and Matt on either side of me. All three guys wrap their muscular arms around me, holding me close and enveloping me in their warmth and strength.

"It's going to be okay," Luke says, pressing a kiss to my hair.

Shane runs a comforting hand up and down my back. "We'll figure it out."

"And whatever happens, we'll deal with it together," Matt says.

I relax against their hard chests, letting their words soothe me. It's not a perfect plan and we all know things will go sideways at some point, but there's not much we can do about it but wait and see. And if it does fall apart and prove to be a temporary romance, I don't want to waste a single second more of it being worried or unhappy.

I extricate myself from the guys and jump to my feet, planting a smile on my face. "Okay, enough of that. How about I make us all some popcorn and we go watch a movie?"

"I like the sound of that," Matt says. "Except I'm picking the movie."

Shane rises to his feet. "I'll get us some wine."

Luke kisses my cheek. "Great idea."

We get our wine and snacks and head into the home theater, where Matt puts on an old 80's comedy. The guys all snuggle up around me on the leather sofa while the movie starts. When we're all settled in together, laughing and cuddling and eating popcorn, my heart feels full again. Maybe this won't last, but for now this thing we have together is perfect.

CHAPTER THIRTY-EIGHT

ALLIE

A MONTH PASSES and the media forgets about me and Luke as they move on to speculating about someone else. All four of us become super busy with work, but we manage to sneak in some time together—both one-on-one and as a group—whenever we can. I'm starting to think maybe this strange relationship we have will actually work out after all.

Then I show up at school and spot a herd of paparazzi waiting outside of it. As I park my car—which still has the warning lights on it, and yes I should have gotten it checked, but I was busy, okay?—they swarm to the fence and snap photos of me, calling out all sorts of questions that I can't make out. But I have a feeling I already know what they're asking about.

I quickly run inside the high school and hope they'll go away if I ignore them. Fat chance, but what else can I do?

I'm nearly to my classroom and only a minute or two late, when I see the principal standing outside the door, his face grim. Oh shit.

"Ms. Chambers, a word please?" he asks.

I swallow the lump in my throat and nod. "Of course, Principal Moore."

He leads me down the now-empty corridors while class starts behind all the doors we pass. My red kitten-toe heels click loudly on the dirty floor underneath us, and I self-consciously yank down my charcoal gray skirt. The entire way to his office I itch to pull out my phone and Google myself or the guys to find out what is going on, but I restrain myself somehow.

Once inside, he gestures for me to sit across from him, as he moves behind his desk. "I'm sure you know what this is about," he says, as he folds his hands on the table.

"Not really, no," I say with a hitch in my voice.

He arches an eyebrow. "It's all over the internet. Photos of you with three actors by a pool, engaging in some sort of... sexual act. With all of them."

"What?" I grab my phone and look it up, and there it is: a picture of me completely naked in the arms of all three guys on the night of Luke's movie premiere. There is no doubt that I'm enjoying attention from all three of them in some way.

Oh my god. This is so much worse than I imagined. "That's not—I mean—I can explain," I sputter.

"I doubt it." He sniffs. "As you know, this is a private school that caters to some of the wealthiest and most powerful people in the city. We have a certain image we must maintain and your lifestyle does not align with that image. We're going to have to let you go."

The world falls out from under my feet, even though I'm sitting down. "No! You can't do that. Please, I love this job and

I've worked here for three years! I'm sure there's something I can do. Maybe I can make a statement or—"

He shakes his head stiffly. "I've already had parents complaining to me about the photos. They don't want you teaching their children and I can't say I blame them."

He makes me feel like some kind of depraved, sex-crazy woman. Like I'm in *The Scarlet Letter* with an A on my chest. Except I didn't cheat. Everything we did was consensual and loving. "My private life isn't your business and has nothing to do with my teaching abilities. You have no right to judge me or fire me for this."

"Unfortunately, I do. Now do I need to call security, or will you get your things and vacate the premises easily?"

I drop my head, completely defeated. "I'll go."

I pack up my things with tears in my eyes, silently saying goodbye to my classroom and my teaching career, then avoid the paparazzi outside and somehow manage to get home. By the time I walk into the house, water is streaming down my face. What am I supposed to do now? I loved that job and I really needed the money. Not to mention, now everyone knows about me and the guys.

Even worse, they aren't home. I wonder if they're facing the backlash of this right now too. Matt might be getting fired from his new role. Shane's TV show might be in the process of getting cancelled. Luke might never get another big movie ever again. And me? I have no idea what I'll do with my life now. No one is going to hire me as a teacher again, not anymore. Not when I'm "Hollywood's Slut," as the tabloids have dubbed me.

I pull out my phone again and see messages from dozens of people and that knot in my stomach only gets tighter. Parker.

My sister. My parents. Oh god, my parents. I can't talk to them right now. I nearly throw my phone across the room, but then it rings. Brooke.

"Are you okay?" she asks, when I pick up the phone.

I let out a choked sob. "No. I just got fired."

"Oh, Allie. I'm so sorry."

"Everything is falling apart." I glance around the kitchen, remembering the guys fighting when the media got a picture of me and Luke. I can only imagine how much worse it will be now. Their careers are going to be ruined. Their friendships will fall apart. I can't let their lives be destroyed because of me. I love them too much to let that happen.

"What are you going to do?" Brooke asks.

"I don't know." My head spins. I can't be here any longer. "I can't do this anymore, Brooke."

"I understand. If there's anything I can do to help let me know."

I draw in a sharp breath. "I need to move out. Right now."

"Of course. Come stay with me. Whatever you need."

"Thanks. I'll be over soon."

"Okay. But...are you sure you want to do this?"

"No, but I think I have to."

After I hang up, I take a moment to write up a note for the guys and then head downstairs to pack my things. My chest aches, my eyes won't stop crying, but I know one thing for certain: I have to get out of here fast before I make anything worse.

CHAPTER THIRTY-NINE

MATT

I ARRIVE HOME at the same time as the other guys, in a parade of expensive cars with pissed-off drivers. We converge in the kitchen and immediately grab some beers from the fridge. It's only ten in the morning but fuck it, this is an emergency.

"I'm assuming you've all heard then," Shane says, as he glances at our grim faces.

I lean against the counter. "Unfortunately. I was in the middle of a script read-through with my new director and had to put it all on hold. I'm not sure I'll even have a part in this movie after today."

Luke clasps a hand on my shoulder. "Damn, I'm sorry. I was meeting with a producer who wanted to cast me in his next action flick. Not sure if that's going to happen now either."

"We also stopped shooting *Talon* for the day once the news got out," Shane says.

I sigh. "Well, we all knew this would blow up in our faces

eventually."

"Yeah, but not like this." Shane glares at his beer as if it were the source of all of our problems. "Not with naked photos of the four of us."

"My agent says if we ignore it and lay low for a while it will blow over in a few days," Luke says.

Shane takes a sip of his beer with a scowl. "And my agent says we're fucked. We're going to lose everything we've worked for all this time. Our careers will be destroyed overnight."

"If that's true then there's nothing we can do about it now," Luke says. "We just have to get through it somehow."

"What about Allie?" I ask. "Fuck, she's going to be so upset when she finds out."

Shane checks the time. "She's still at work. We have a few hours to figure out how to handle this before she gets home."

I spot something on the countertop. A note with Allie's handwriting. "No, she's not. Check this out."

I grab the note and read it with dread in my stomach.

This isn't working out. I'm sorry, but this is over.

Oh shit.

Without a word, I turn to the other guys and hand them the note.

"Did she just break up with us?" Luke asks.

"I think so." Shane crumples up his empty beer can. "Fuck, I knew this was a mistake from the beginning!"

I glare at him. "How can you say that?"

"Do you disagree?" He spreads his arms. "Look what it's doing to us."

Luke runs a hand through his hair. "Shit, maybe he's right. Maybe we never should have gotten into this mess."

"Maybe not, but we're in it now," I say. "And I don't know about you guys, but I don't want to lose Allie."

"Neither do I," Luke says.

"I don't want to lose her either, but I don't see any way out of this," Shane says.

I punch my fist. "Then we fight for her. Allie is worth it."

"All right," Luke says. "For her, I'll do whatever it takes."

Shane nods. "Agreed."

I let out a long breath, relief easing the tension in my shoulders. Our friendship could have been destroyed if this conversation had gone a different way. Our relationship with Allie could have been over too. But instead, we're all willing to give up anything for her.

I grin at the two of them. "Then let's go get her back."

We head down the stairs like three soldiers charging into battle. When we get to her door, she's throwing her clothes into a suitcase. Her eyes are all red and puffy from crying, and at the sight of us she looks like she might burst into tears again.

"Don't try to change my mind," she says, before any of us can get a word in, while pulling more clothes off her hangars. "I'm moving out. I've decided it's for this best. We tried this and it didn't work and I'm going to leave before I make everything worse between all of us."

"We don't want you to move out," I say. "We want to make this work."

"How?" She shakes her head. "Your careers are going to be ruined because of me. Hell, my career is already ruined."

"What do you mean?" Luke asks.

"I got fired." A soft sob escapes her throat. "Yep. Turns out naked photos of me with three famous guys doesn't work for the school's reputation." She sniffs. "I'll be lucky if anyone ever hires me again."

"I'm so sorry," I say, as I move toward her to give her a hug. But she steps back and raises a hand to stop me.

"It's my fault. I got greedy. Who did I really think I was, thinking I could have three boyfriends? Especially ones as sexy and amazing as each of you. I'd be lucky to have just *one* of you, but oh no, I had to go for all three and ruin everything." She shakes her head furiously as she shoves her clothes in her luggage.

"You're not greedy," Luke says. "We're the ones who wanted to share you. And we enjoyed it."

"But it's my fault the photo got out!" she blurts out.

"How so?" I ask.

She drops her head. "It was Parker. He came to see me a month ago at school and wanted me back. I got the feeling he wasn't going to leave me alone, but then I never heard anything else so I thought I was safe. But he must have followed me back here and spied on us together after Luke's premiere. Then he sold the photo to the press." She raises her head and glances between all of us with sadness in her eyes. "All of this is my fault. I'm sorry."

"It is not your fault," Shane says.

"Not at all," I add. "And our relationship would have gotten out to the media eventually."

"How do you know it was Parker?" Luke asks.

She holds up her phone. "He sent me a text saying if I get back together with him then he'll say the photo was a fake."

"Is that where you're going?" Shane asks, his eyes narrowing.

Her eyes widen. "No way! I'd never get back with him. I was going to stay with Brooke."

Shane clenches his fists. "That asshole. I'm going to kill him."

"Not if I get to him first," Luke says, his jaw clenched.

"No killing," I say, rolling my eyes. "Yes, he deserves it, but we're in enough trouble already."

Luke huffs. "Fine, but he and I are going to have a long talk. With my fists and his face."

"You don't need to worry about Parker," Allie says. "I'm going to see if Brooke can take some legal action against him. Invasion of privacy. A restraining order. Something." She sighs as she zips up her full luggage. "I don't know what else I can do to fix this though. I'm sorry."

"Don't be sorry," I say. "None of this is your fault, and yes things are a mess right now, but we'll get through it. Together."

"How?" she asks.

"This will all blow over in a few days," Luke says. "I know it seems terrible now, but soon enough another scandal will sweep through Hollywood and everyone will forget all about this."

"And you don't need to worry about work," Shane says. "We'll take care of you."

"I can't let you do that," Allie says. "Besides, I *like* working. I don't want to be some trophy wife. I want my own life and my own career."

Shane's brow furrows. "Then we'll find you something else. We have connections and we won't stop until you get a new job you love."

She sighs and doesn't look convinced. "But what about your TV show? And Luke and Matt's movies?"

Luke shrugs. "Maybe the extra publicity will help them. Who knows? The fact is, we don't care. We'd give up all of our careers if it meant keeping you."

"Allie, we don't want to lose you," I say. "No matter what happens."

Shane nods. "It doesn't matter what the media says or what happens to us, because all three of us are willing to risk our careers and everything else to be with you, Allie."

"You are?" she asks.

I step forward and take her hand. "Allie, I've never felt this way about any other girl in my life. You're the only one I've ever wanted something serious with and I'll do anything to keep you." I pull her close. "I love you."

Her eyes fill up with tears again as she squeezes my hand. "Oh, Matt. I love you too."

Luke moves in close, taking her other hand and turning her toward him. "I thought I'd never find love again after Lana broke my heart. I wasn't sure I'd ever move on from that. But you proved me wrong. I love you, Allie."

She laughs softly, like she can't believe this is happening. "I love you too, Luke."

Shane steps between us, resting his hands on Allie's waist. "I tried to push you away. I tried to keep you out of my heart. But I loved you from the moment you first walked in that door and I can't deny it any longer."

Her smile is so bright it lights up the entire room. "Shane, I love you too."

He kisses her first, then Luke and I take turns kissing her next. I taste the salty tears on her lips and suck them away. No more sadness now. Only love.

"Does that mean you're staying?" I ask.

"Yes, I'll stay," she says, giving us a weary yet hopeful smile. "I'm scared about what people will think and what will happen to all of us, but I know we'll get through it if we stick together."

"Thank god," Shane says.

He crushes his mouth against hers as his hands circle her waist. Luke and I press in on either side of her, kissing her neck while stroking her back, gripping her hips, and squeezing her ass. She's wearing a sexy white button-up shirt over a gray skirt and all I can think about is getting them off her.

It's time to show her how much we all love her.

CHAPTER FORTY

ALLIE

A FEW MINUTES ago I was bawling my eyes out as I packed my bags and prepared to leave the house forever. Then all three guys admitted they loved me and wanted me to stay—and I realized I loved them all too. It felt so good saying it out loud and not giving a crap what other people think about our relationship. None of that matters because what I have with all three guys is not only real—it's perfect.

As they all kiss and fondle me I can only close my eyes and appreciate how lucky I am. Each guy is my dream man in a different way. Matt is funny, charming, and has a good heart. Luke is protective, warm, and full of inner strength. Shane is brooding, smart, and secretly a big softie. Together, they make me feel bold, confident, and happy in a way I've never been before.

Matt slowly unbuttons my blouse, while Luke's mouth kisses every inch of skin his brother reveals. Shane helps remove the shirt from my shoulders, and then they unzip the side of my skirt and let it hit the floor. A rush of cool air touches my bare skin, but they don't stop there. As their lips caress me all over, Luke unhooks my bra and frees my breasts, while Matt drags my panties off me, and Shane removes my heels one by one.

Now I'm standing naked before them, not just in body but in heart and soul. Each man takes a long look at me, their eyes shining with love and something like protectiveness. Something that says, *mine*. Except there's no jealousy or competition, and when the three of them nod at each other, it's as if they're reaching an agreement.

"Today it's all about you," Shane says to me.

"We're going to make you feel so good," Matt says.

My pulse races with desire. "You always do."

"Yes, but this time, we're all going to be inside you," Luke says. "If you want that, that is?"

My heartbeat speeds up at the thought of finally experiencing this fantasy I've dreamed of ever since I saw the three guys. "Yes, please."

The three of them ease me onto the bed and spread my legs wide, while my heart races with eager anticipation. Each brother moves to my breasts, then takes a nipple and begins teasing pleasure out of it. At the same time, Shane's head moves between my thighs. The first stroke of his tongue is so good it makes me moan, and I can't imagine how things could get even better than this moment with all three of their mouths on me. But I know it will.

I slide my hands into the brothers' beautiful, thick hair, gripping them tight as Shane's tongue continues its slow exploration. Matt and Luke lavish the same amount of attention on my breasts, my neck, and my arms, making me feel pampered and loved all over. A warm glow spreads throughout me as they worship my body, growing hotter and hotter with each touch, until my thighs quiver, my fingers tighten, and I cry out each of their names.

But it's not enough. I want to be connected to them—all of them.

"I need you," I tell them. "Please."

Shane rises up and gives me a smoldering look, then nudges his cock at my entrance. Slipping inside a tiny bit, just to tease me. "You want this?"

"Yes. All of you." I lift my hips, trying to get more of him, but he holds back. He slides the tip slowly along my slick skin, driving me wild.

"We should do what the lady wants," Matt says, with a naughty grin.

"Fine, but it's my turn in back," Luke says.

My breath catches at the thought, but before I can respond, Shane lifts me up into his arms and slides inside me at the same time. I moan and cling to him as he fills me up, while Luke lies flat on the bed behind us. My mouth finds Shane's lips and I taste my desire on him, but then I turn to watch the brothers over my shoulder. Luke slowly rubs lube onto his own long shaft, while Matt moves close behind me and Shane, planting a soft kiss on my shoulder. As his mouth leaves a hot trail across my neck, his slippery finger enters my tight hole to begin getting me ready.

I'm pressed between their warm, powerful bodies, and Shane begins rocking up into me. Matt's finger slowly works in and out, while he pulls my hair to the side and presses a kiss to the back of my neck. When I relax against him, he slides another finger into me, widening me and stretching me, although I know nothing he does will fully prepare me for Luke's size. God, I can't wait.

"She's ready," Matt says. He captures my chin and turns my face toward him, then captures my mouth in a passionate kiss, before stepping back.

Shane slides out of me, but then he and Matt take me in their arms again and lower me into position on Luke's body. Together they slowly ease me down onto him, while Luke holds my hips to help guide me. The pressure at my back entrance is intense, but it's amazing too. I suck in a breath as his entire head pushes inside.

"Oh god, it feels so good," Luke says. I'm facing away from him, still clinging to Shane and Matt, but the pleasure in his voice matches what I'm feeling too.

"You doing okay?" Shane asks me, his brow furrowed. I love his concern, even if I'm totally fine. Way better than fine, actually.

"Yes," I manage to get out. "More."

Luke sinks deeper inside me and the mix of pain and pleasure is so strong I almost can't stand it, but at the same time, I want even more. I want to feel him fully sheathed inside me, and then I want the other men to join us. Only then will I be satisfied.

I push down and then he's all the way in, my butt resting on his hips, and we both let out a moan. I rock up and down a bit on Luke at first, letting my body grow accustomed to his size, before beckoning the other two men forward.

"You sure you can take all three of us?" Matt asks.

"I'm sure." I've never done it before, but we'll make it work. Just like we'll make this relationship work.

While Luke holds me in place, Shane moves between my

thighs and rubs himself against me once, then pushes inside again. The exquisite fullness is unlike anything else in the world, and I know the only thing that can feel better is if Matt joins us too.

When Shane's all the way inside me, he cups my breasts and gazes into my eyes. "I love it like this, with you pinned between us."

"I love it when you're both inside me," I say, stroking his face. "But I want Matt too."

"And you'll have me," Matt says, as he moves beside me, giving a nice view of his muscular, naked body.

I take his cock in my hand, giving it one long stroke while wetting my lips. His nostrils flare as I open my mouth, welcoming him inside. He slides his hand into my hair, tangling his fingers in the red strands, as I give his shaft a slow lick, then look up at him with a dirty smile.

"Fuck, that's hot," Shane says.

"No kidding," Luke says from behind me.

I grin and then take Matt between my lips, making him groan. The other guys watch as I slowly suck and lick him, while they seem to get harder inside me somehow. I don't blame them. I'm touching all three of my men at once, giving them each pleasure while receiving it from them at the same time. The thought alone is enough to nearly send me off the edge already.

The three men begin moving and it somehow gets even better. Slowly at first, finding the right pace and best angles, learning how the four of us fit together. Soon the guys find the right rhythm and our bodies rock back and forth together, sliding in and out of me in tandem, and the sound of our cries and moans becomes the best song I've ever heard. All three of them are inside me and against me and I've never felt so deliciously possessed in my entire life, while at the same time feeling so powerful. These men are mine, not only their bodies, but their hearts. I own them as much as they own me. And I never plan on letting them go.

My climax is so strong I lose all control of myself, giving myself to the men completely. I let them take hold of me and ride out their pleasure inside me, as the orgasm consumes me. It's stronger than everything I've ever felt before, encompassing my entire body, setting every nerve ending on fire—and it doesn't end. It keeps going and going until I scream, and that's when the guys finally join me. Matt first, releasing himself inside my mouth with a rush of wet heat. Then Luke and Shane at nearly the same time, both of them surging inside me as they let go and lose control.

We collapse onto the bed together in a tangle of sweaty limbs and naked skin and pounding hearts. For minutes, all we can do is cling to each other. The men lovingly stroke me all over, while I run my hands over each of them, and my heart is so happy it nearly hurts. I know that whatever happens to us we'll get through it, because we're stronger together.

Shane nuzzles his head against my neck. "You're incredible."

"I love you," I say, smiling at each of them. "All of you."

"You better," Matt says, tightening his arm around my waist. "Because you're stuck with us."

Luke winks. "And we're kind of a package deal now."

EPILOGUE
ALLIE

SOFT HOLIDAY MUSIC plays in the background while I bring a freshly-baked platter of cookies into the living room. I set them down on the dining room table beside the other delicious food, most of which was catered by a fancy service Shane's assistant recommended, but some of which I did myself. I sometimes let the guys pamper me with their fancy chefs and cleaning crews, but only so much. And you better believe I decorated the house myself, with their help of course. Hence the holly, mistletoe, lights, and Christmas decorations draped around the living room and kitchen, along with the front of the house and the back patio. We even have fake snow. Hey, I did say I love holidays, after all.

"Mm," Matt says, grabbing a tree-shaped cookie off the tray. Tonight he's wearing an ugly Christmas sweater with reindeer that somehow does nothing to detract from his natural sexiness. "Your cookies are my favorite."

"I know. Don't worry, I saved you some extra ones." I

nudge him. "Now if we could only get your brother to eat one."

"Yeah, right," Matt says, with a snort.

Luke grins and plucks a snowflake-shaped cookie from the platter. "For Allie, I'll have one, just because it's Christmas Eve. But only one." He slides a hand along his stomach, raising his burgundy shirt to give me a tantalizing glimpse of his abs. "Don't want all this hard work to be for nothing."

I shake my head with a smile, while Shane comes over and grabs a cookie too. He's wearing a black suit and tie, looking every inch the dashing host of the party. As he bites into my cookie, I grin. I've won them all over it seems. Who could have predicted it when I moved in with these guys a few months ago?

Brooke moves beside me with a grin, wearing a low-cut black dress, her nails dark green tonight. "Nice little party."

"Yeah, it is." I gaze across the small crowd of people in the living room and kitchen. Only close friends and family were invited, specifically the ones who know about our unconventional relationship and are okay with it. Including my sister Kristen and her husband, who were surprisingly supportive of me after the big media blowup. My parents were invited too, but they're still getting used to the idea of me dating three men. I'm sure they'll come around eventually though.

The big scandal about the photos died down after a few weeks, partly thanks to Luke's ex-wife, Lana. She got arrested after she crashed her car into the set of her new movie, breaking the director's leg in the process. Turns out she was high on meth at the time. No one cared about us after that. Surprisingly, none of the guys' careers suffered from the scandal either. I chalk it up to the fact that men can get away with things that woman get labelled a "slut" for, but I'm still happy for them.

As for me? I got a job as a librarian, which I love even more than teaching. I spend my entire day with books and, even better, help people discover new ones. When they hired me I worried they'd care about my reputation, but the other librarians shrugged it off—as long as I agreed to have the guys do some fundraising events for the library now and then. In fact, one of them—a brunette named Sienna who loves books as much as I do—has already become a good friend and is currently flirting with a guy who worked with Matt at the bar. I hope she gets lucky tonight.

And Parker, well, Brooke threatened to sue him, and the three guys had a little talk with him about leaving us alone. No one's heard from him since. Thank god.

Brooke hands me a perfectly wrapped gift with a silver ribbon. "Merry Christmas. Spoiler alert, I got you a monthly planner because I figure with three boyfriends you'll need some mad organizational skills to keep up with all of them."

I laugh. "Thank you. That's exactly what I need."

It really is. I can barely wrap my head around dating three men at once, especially three busy actors. The sleeping arrangements alone make my brain hurt sometimes. At the moment the men trade off having me sleep in their beds, so they each get two nights a week with me. The seventh night is spent in my bed, usually with at least two of them beside me. Sometimes three.

Somehow the four of us are making this strange relationship work without jealousy or any other problems. I think it helps that the three guys care about each other too. Their friendship has only grown stronger in the last few months.

As the party continues into the night, I spot Brooke and Hannah talking in a corner, both of them looking beautiful as their eyes linger on the other and their mouths slip into flirty smiles. They're perfect for each other, like I knew they would be. My work here is done.

As I smooth my frosty pale blue gown, I gaze at my three men standing together by the Christmas tree, laughing at something Matt said. Love swells inside my chest at the sight of them, each one so handsome, smart, and strong. I still can't believe how lucky I am to have ended up with them.

After the party ends and everyone leaves, when we're all a little drunk and way too full, the four of us stand around the Christmas tree. Luke pops a bottle of champagne and pours a glass for each of us, while Matt finishes up another of my cookies. Shane then raises his glass in a toast.

"I think we can all agree we have a lot to celebrate this year," he says. "Matt's filming a new role in a very promising movie. Luke's latest movie killed it at the box office and they're already doing a sequel. I managed to not only save my show, but boost the ratings too. And none of us could have done it without this amazing woman." He turns toward me and slides an arm around my waist. "Allie, we are so lucky you came into our lives. You're the best Christmas gift we could have asked for."

"To Allie," Matt says, raising his glass.

"To Allie," Luke agrees.

I blush as I smile at them. "Thank you, but I'm the lucky one here. The three of you took me in when I had nowhere else to go, when I was a total mess. Parker killed my confidence and made me think no man would ever want me again. But somehow all three of you made me believe I was worthy of love, even when things became difficult and it seemed like the world would never accept us. Thank you, thank you, thank you."

Luke rests a warm hand on my back. "You're the one who improved our lives when you moved in."

"You changed all three of us for the better," Matt says, pressing a kiss to my cheek.

Shane nods. "You're ours and all we want is to make you happy."

"As long as I get to make each of you happy in return," I say.

"Oh, you do," Matt says. "Very much."

We clink glasses and take a sip of champagne. I lean over and kiss each guy, tasting the bubbly alcohol on their lips. I'm about to ask them to join me in my room, when Matt glances at his watch.

"It's past midnight," he says, with a devilish grin. "Can we give Allie her presents now?"

Shane shrugs. "I don't see why not."

Luke's lips curl into a warm smile. "Yes, I can't wait any longer."

I raise an eyebrow at them. "What's this about?"

Matt takes my hand. "Come on, we'll show you."

The three guys lead me toward the garage, of all places, while my curiosity grows. Inside, we pass by the other guys' cars, where I discover my ancient and barely-running blue Ford Focus is gone—now replaced by another car. A bright red Corvette Stingray.

"Oh my god," I say, then cover my mouth with my hands. "Is it for me?"

Luke grins at my reaction. "We couldn't let you drive that clunker anymore."

"You told me a month ago this was your dream car," Matt says. "Do you like it?"

"I love it!" Giddiness bursts inside me, but then I bite my lip. "No, this is way too much. I didn't get you anything so big or fancy for Christmas. I can't accept this."

"Don't worry," Shane says. "We all chipped in to get it for you and we don't expect anything in return. We just wanted you to have it."

Luke wraps an arm around me. "Allie, you're ours now, and we're going to take care of you."

"That means giving you everything you could ever want," Matt adds.

I give them a hesitant smile. "Okay, as long as you don't go *too* crazy."

"Hey, Shane wanted to get you a pink Lamborghini, but we talked him out of that," Matt says, with a wink.

Shane flashes a sly grin. "Next time."

I laugh and run around my new, beautiful car to check it out from all angles. I can't believe it's actually mine. "Wow. Thank you so much. I really do love the car. I have to admit, I do like being spoiled by you three sometimes."

"Good," Shane says. "Because you have an entire lifetime of being spoiled to look forward to."

"Is that so?" I ask playfully.

"I think it's time for her other present," Luke says, with a knowing gleam in his eye.

The guys lead me back to the Christmas tree with secretive smiles. Once we're surrounded by twinkling lights and the smell of pine, Shane drops to one knee, making me gasp. The other guys follow, kneeling in front of me like knights waiting for me to bless them.

"What are you doing?" I ask, my heart pounding faster. A flicker of hope and excitement bubbles within me, but I don't dare think they might actually be proposing. That assumption didn't work out so well for me last time, after all.

"Allie, we love you so much," Matt says, and his charming smile makes me believe this might actually be happening. For real this time.

"And we never want to be without you." Luke pulls out a ring box. He pops it open, revealing a giant diamond ring. And I do mean *giant*.

Shane gazes up at me with his piercing blue eyes and asks, "Allie, will you marry us?"

I let out a little squee, as shock and happiness rush through me. It's really, truly happening. They're proposing to me. And it's not a trick, not a dream, and not a proposal for someone else.

But then reality sets in and I ask, "Is marriage with the three of you even possible?"

"There's a small country in the Caribbean called Andora that lets people have group marriages," Shane says. "It's a former British colony run by a queen and her three husbands."

I let out a surprised laugh. "Wow, clearly we need to move there."

"Maybe we'll buy a second house there someday," Luke says.

"Then yes, I'll marry you." I let out a joyful laugh, even as happy tears fill my eyes. "I love you all so much."

Each guy wears a handsome smile while they place the engagement ring on my finger, before rising to their feet and wrapping me in their arms. As I snuggle up against them, I feel truly content, like this is exactly where I'm meant to be.

Matt pulls back and flashes me a wicked grin. "Come on, let's open some more presents. Wait 'til you see what I got Shane this year."

Shane groans. "It better not be another prank gift."

"Ooh, like the one from last year?" Luke asks.

My heart warms as they continue teasing each other while we sit around the Christmas tree and unwrap some presents. I never imagined I could ever be so happy, let alone with three men. No matter what happens, or what society thinks of us, we'll get through it and come out even stronger. We've found our true family together—and I know it will last forever.

ACKNOWLEDGMENTS

Reverse harem is a new genre for me, but I'm really excited to be writing in it! Many thanks to the following people who helped me with this book along the way:

-My beta readers, Jessica Love, Lissa Hawley, and Lisa Mandina. This book is so much better thanks to all of you!

-My RH ladies, Eva Chase, Lidiya Foxglove, and Sarah Piper. I wouldn't want to go on this journey with anyone but you three!

-My awesome friend, Sybil Bartel, for convincing me to leave in the naughty stuff!

-My cover designer, KassiJean Designs, and my photographer, Lindee Robinson, for making my cover so beautiful!

-My agent, Kate Testerman, who didn't freak out when I told her what I was writing next!

-My family, for putting up with my crazy writer brain. I really hope you're not reading this book...

-And, as always, to my lovely husband Gary Briggs, for

being the best guy ever. Thanks for letting me write whatever I want and supporting me through everything.

ABOUT THE AUTHOR

Elizabeth Briggs is the *New York Times* bestselling author of paranormal and fantasy romance. She graduated from UCLA with a degree in Sociology and has worked for an international law firm, mentored teens in writing, and volunteered with dog rescue groups. Now she's a full-time geek who lives in Los Angeles with her family and a pack of fluffy dogs.

Visit Elizabeth's website: www.elizabethbriggs.net

Printed in Great Britain
by Amazon